THREE POLITICAL TALES
FROM MEDIEVAL GERMANY

Studies in German Literature, Linguistics, and Culture

THREE POLITICAL TALES FROM MEDIEVAL GERMANY

DUKE ERNST, *HENRY OF KEMPTEN*, AND *REYNARD THE FOX*

Translated and with an introduction by
Brian Murdoch

CAMDEN HOUSE
Rochester, New York

Copyright © 2024 Brian Murdoch

All Rights Reserved. Except as permitted under current legislation, no part of this work may be photocopied, stored in a retrieval system, published, performed in public, adapted, broadcast, transmitted, recorded, or reproduced in any form or by any means, without the prior permission of the copyright owner.

First published 2024
by Camden House

Camden House is an imprint of Boydell & Brewer Inc.
668 Mt. Hope Avenue, Rochester, NY 14620, USA
and of Boydell & Brewer Limited
PO Box 9, Woodbridge, Suffolk IP12 3DF, UK
www.boydellandbrewer.com

ISBN-13: 978-1-64014-185-8

Library of Congress Cataloging-in-Publication Data
CIP data is available from the Library of Congress.

CONTENTS

Preface	vii
Introduction (with Bibliographical Notes)	ix

Duke Ernst   1

1	The Young Nobleman	3
2	The Rebel	22
3	The Exile	33
4	The Citadel of the Cranes	38
5	A Perilous Journey	61
6	A New King and New Challenges	70
7	The Crusader	83
8	The Penitent Restored	89

Konrad von Würzburg, *Henry of Kempten*   95

Heinrich, *Reynard the Fox*   109

1	The Fox and the Cockerel	111
2	The Fox and the Bluetit	114
3	The Fox and the Crow	115

4	The Fox and the Dogs	117
5	The Fox and the Tomcat	118
6	The Fox and the Wolf	120
7	The Fox and the She-Wolf	121
8	The Wolf and the Ham	122
9	The Wolf and the Wine	124
10	The Fox and the Ass (incomplete)	126
11	Kunin	127
12	The Wolf's Tonsure	129
13	The Wolf Goes Fishing	131
14	The Fox, the Wolf, and the Well	134
15	A Day in Court	138
16	The Rape of the She-Wolf	141
17	The Ants and the Lion	143
18	The Great Assembly and the Saintly Chicken	145
19	The Bear and the Honey	149
20	The Tomcat and the Mice	152
21	The Badger, the Fox, and the Sick Lion	154
22	The Elephant and the Camel	161
23	The Murder of the King	163

PREFACE

This collection offers translations of three tales, originally in verse, from medieval Germany. The first—whose author is anonymous—is the story of Duke Ernst (*Herzog Ernst*); the second, by the well-known and prolific writer Konrad von Würzburg, is that of Henry of Kempten (*Heinrich von Kempten*; the work is also known as *Otto mit dem Bart*); and the third, by an author of whom we know very little, but who names himself as Heinrich, is about a figure who is very well known, Reynard the Fox (*Reinhart Fuchs*). The three tales, two about knights and adventure and one about the trickery of a cunning fox, are all entertaining, but they are also all essentially political, and their messages are not exclusively medieval. The first two, although exciting and adventurous (and Ernst in particular travels and meets exotic and strange creatures), both show young men in conflict with the state, or its embodiment in the emperor, and both men learn the necessity of compromise in order to maintain the stability of the state. The third story first shows us the familiar fox up to his usual pranks but then becomes darker as the fox becomes the most untrustworthy adviser at the court of the lion king in a disturbing fable about the acquisition of power.

For help in the production of this book, several votes of thanks are due, first to the many students with whom I read and discussed these texts over a good number of years at the University of Stirling. In the production of this book, I owe a great debt of gratitude to the two readers, who made informed, detailed, and extremely useful comments; this is an aspect of academic work that deserves much credit and thanks (although in the time-honored but quite genuine formula, any remaining errors are my responsibility!). My professional and my personal thanks go, too, to the indefatigable Jim Walker, whose expertise, advice, and endless patience have meant a great deal to me over the many years we have worked together, when he has supported me in publishing books on both modern and medieval literature.

Most importantly, of course, thanks are due to Ursula, my wife, who has lived with this material, read and reread, and generally put up with random medieval characters for so long. This book is dedicated to her.

BM
Stirling, 2023

INTRODUCTION
(WITH BIBLIOGRAPHICAL NOTES)

The Political Focus

The three medieval German texts translated here are all political in that they each demonstrate just how precarious even a supposedly rigidly organized society—such as the Holy Roman Empire—can be. All three of them are designed to entertain, and they do it well, but in addition, they all instruct. Two of them are adventure stories, in different styles, but both with a message about the care needed to prevent the escalation of violence that can lead any society into a descent into chaos. The third is a bleak illustration of how things can be manipulated by the unscrupulous and can end in disaster. The three works are in very different styles. The first, *Duke Ernst*, begins with a political conflict but develops into what is almost a fantasy novel as the central character goes (most certainly boldly) to strange places outside the known world and meets (sometimes fights with, but also learns from) strange and alien creatures before returning to the world from which he set out. The second, *Henry of Kempten*, is ostensibly a novella about chivalric bravery, but it is set in a prechivalric period and is really about the ease with which an initially apparently trivial incident can escalate toward a major disaster that is here only just avoided. The third is an animal fable, part of an extensive tradition as far as genre and theme are concerned and involving the fox we know as Reynard; it is comfortably familiar for the first part, at least, but it develops into a very dark political tale indeed and ends with the death of a king.

The first two works in particular have at their center the concept of empire, *rîche*, and it is perhaps necessary to comment here that these are medieval texts and that the notions of empire and imperialism (and the overlaps with colonialism), not to say the very word *Reich*, have in recent centuries acquired overtones that they did not have in the medieval context. This does not mean that the presentation of these texts implies a defense in the modern world of medieval or of any other autocratic rule, and the emperors in the first two works are themselves, interestingly, very far from perfect; but on a more basic level, in these works what is, like it or not, usually called the "Holy Roman Empire" connotes a functioning political unit, the state. Its manifestation in the Middle Ages of course had enormous flaws and inequities, which history has been working on ever since with a greater or lesser degree of success—political evolution progresses very slowly and jerkily indeed. These works all make the point, however, that the alternative to political organization was (and in spite of the changes over the centuries still is) chaos and anarchy. Sometimes a potential crisis can be averted if there is some goodwill or moral and political awareness present. But this is not always the case, and the last of these three works shows how a whole political structure can be brought down at the hands of an unscrupulous and entirely self-centered but clever opportunist, who, among other attributes, tells lies frequently and fluently. The author of *Reynard the Fox* regularly interrupts his narrative to remind us expressly that evil deeds happen and will go on happening.

Middle High German literature—which was written in the linguistic period that ran roughly speaking from the end of the eleventh century until the start of the sixteenth, and that had a literary peak in the thirteenth—contains several very well-known political sagas, often based on an earlier Germanic age. The German *Nibelungenlied*, the Song of the Nibelungen, shows us the fall of an entire state when a disruptive influence, Siegfried, is allowed in. Pragmatic strategies to maintain stability are demonstrated in the equally impressive epic *Kudrun*, in which dominant women play a controlling role, albeit with the help of one old warrior whose radical solution to ensure long-term submission is to slaughter all the children of the defeated enemy. The focus of the three Middle High German works translated here, and the reason for placing them together, is also essentially political. Two are also set in earlier times, though not quite as far back as the *Nibelungenlied*, and the third is a fable in which animals behave as bestially as humans to show us what human nature is actually like. All three, however, are well-told tales. *Duke Ernst* is an adventure story, that by Konrad is a gem of conciseness, and both are fast paced and exciting, designed to catch one's interest. Heinrich's version of the tale of Reynard has some well-known fables in it, but any familiarity gives way to horror by the end. The three texts may well have spoken most directly to an aristocratic contemporary audience, but the message in each is more general and, in some respects, uncomfortably modern.

Duke Ernst

The anonymous medieval German tale *Duke Ernst* is a long narrative (6,022 lines in rhymed couplets) about a German aristocratic warrior who is much involved in fighting, sometimes against alien creatures, but who also learns the important lesson that although it is possible to inherit or to acquire by family connections a high position within a state (in his own case, the Holy Roman Empire), such a position must also be earned. What makes the story not just important but also interesting is that he learns his lesson partly in the perfectly real world of the Holy Roman Empire and its neighboring lands, in a quasi-historical context that is linked with actual events in the tenth century, and partly in lands that are located off—or at least right on the unexplored edges of—the map. Initially a privileged nobleman, Ernst is caught up in events that cause a civil war and set him against the emperor himself. The internal politics are interesting, as a relative of the ruler poisons his mind against the young duke (although the writer is very clear on his sympathies, which are with Ernst, the situation is nevertheless perfectly plausible, and Ernst is young and impetuous) and suggests a preemptive strike, ostensibly to save the state from chaos. To break a stalemate in a conflict that was not of his making, but that he has made worse by killing his powerful accuser (and very nearly the emperor himself), and that he cannot win, Ernst flees from the empire and fights alongside or against a range of peculiar beings, some taken from the pages of Pliny's *Natural History* and similar sources. We meet sciapods, cyclops (Arimaspi), crane-headed men (as well as some malevolent but apparently genuinely avian cranes as such), pygmies, panotii (long-eared people), giants, and so on. All these strange creatures add interest, but the lesson that Ernst slowly learns is still a political one: how to exercise power honorably within a given (and accepted) political construct. The anonymous writer uses techniques that are almost filmic on some occasions, and on others he plays with the audience, but the special features of the strange creatures are interesting rather than vitally important, except insofar as they force the hero to think up strategies (often simply to launch a bold attack) to defeat them, as every good general must. *Herzog* in German and *duke* in English both mean military leader. At length, having worked his passage, as it were, he returns to the real world, is pardoned, and takes up a useful role within the empire.

We have no idea who wrote or reworked the medieval poem *Duke Ernst*. It used to be classified (regularly, though not invariably) in German literary histories as a "*Spielmannsepos*," minstrel epic, grouped (although transmissions and chronologies are extremely confused) with some other more or less contemporary pieces—not always the same ones, and ones that are not always very similar anyway. No one was ever entirely clear on what the word *Spielmannsepos* implied, and although the wandering minstrel idea dies hard, the writers were probably clerics at a court, and the term is (rightly) now not much used. It was regularly placed in quotation marks at an early stage and was already described as "*durchaus problematisch*," thoroughly problematic, in a standard bibliographical introduction to the supposed genre published in the 1960s (Walter Johannes Schröder, *Spielmannsepik* [Stuttgart: Metzler, 1962], 1). The genre was ostensibly style-based, focusing upon shared but varying features: heroic, burlesque, religious, legendary, and courtly, plus the motifs of disguise and trickery. Other works might have been added to the group—and indeed sometimes were—these including Heinrich's *Reinhart Fuchs*. Our poem was, contrariwise, sometimes bracketed instead with heroic epics like the *Nibelungenlied*.

Duke Ernst is in some respects the equivalent of the modern fantasy or even science-fiction novel, since the central character moves away from the known world, but it remains above all else, as some critics have indeed noted, a political adventure story. At all events we are not in a world of knight-errantry, even though the writer or adapter of this version has tried to lay a certain chivalric veneer on it all, although chivalry itself was probably always to some extent a hopeful fiction in a world of precarious military power–balancing. If the text is concerned principally with aristocratic (even autocratic) rulers, two things nevertheless remain in the mind: the abstract notion of the state, which is voiced so often; and the implicit need to protect what may be seen as the ordinary people by establishing stability as far as possible. The modern German translation of the work in the popular Reclam series, incidentally, tends to translate the word for empire or state (*rîche*) as *Kaiser* (emperor), and this is potentially misleading. Of course the two terms are, in the abstract, political-philosophical terms very closely interlinked; but it is better to distinguish them, as the medieval poet does, and in any case they do not in reality always coincide. Ernst's Emperor Otto, though capable of being misled by advisers related to him and jealous of the young duke, is in the last analysis (and is presented as) an effective ruler. Another Emperor Otto appears in Konrad's novella (the relationship of either of them to historical figures is confusing), and he is presented by the narrator as unpleasant, but he still represents order, and it is his role rather than his character that matters more. In *Duke Ernst*, we are told before the troubles that this Emperor Otto has established a great peace, a *pax Saxonica* (Otto the Great, the first of three emperors with that name in the tenth century, was from Saxony, though the word in the text seems to mean all of Germany), and that his writ ran over a vast area. The peace is disturbed only when the all-too-believable idea is put into Otto's head that the young Ernst (known at this stage better to the audience than to the emperor) might be after his position. Ernst has to learn various skills in diplomacy, and even when he embarks on his adventures abroad, he is not always successful. For example, he causes the death of an Indian princess he is trying to save (although he does preserve her from what she herself sees as a fate worse than that death). But in the long term the adventures he has to face give him both military and political skills, and he fights for the right as far as this can be determined, so that when he returns, he is not only no longer a threat but can also take up a useful place within the state.

 The work falls into two interlocking parts: the first shows the rise and fall of a privileged young man within a given political construct, based on the Holy Roman Empire under Otto the Great, and then at the end completes this part with his restoration, thus enclosing the second part, the adventures. The idea of the rebellion of the young man against the emperor has more than one historical parallel (Otto against Liudolf of Swabia; a later emperor, Konrad II, against Ernst of Swabia), but here the young man Ernst inherits the duchy of Bavaria. When his widowed mother marries Otto, the emperor, Ernst's rise to a position of power and influence within the state is too rapid for one of the emperor's closest and most powerful advisers, Henry of the Rhine, who is a blood relative of the ruler, whereas Ernst's connection is through marriage. Otto, incidentally, has been married before and has children to ensure the succession, so that is not a question here. Henry is count palatine (*Pfalzgraf*, palsgrave, a Carolingian title for a very high-ranking royal adviser, almost a deputy to the emperor), who claims, motivated here (we are told by our narrator) by the devil, and presumably really by jealousy, that Ernst is plotting to take over the empire. Carefully keeping Ernst's mother out of the picture, Henry of the Rhine plays on Ernst's quite genuine popularity to make his claim look plausible. Ernst is forced to fight back and, after some failed diplomatic attempts at reconciliation, finds himself out on a limb. In a bold raid in which he could very well have killed the emperor himself in his rage, he manages to kill Count Henry, while the emperor barely escapes. The situation has now escalated enormously, such that Henry's original lies about Ernst's insurrection have now effectively proved themselves. Small beginnings and internal jealousies have led almost to the removal of the head of the state. Ernst is never blamed by the narrator, but objectively the political implications are clear. Ernst incurs the guilt of attacking and nearly killing the emperor, which is tantamount to an attack on the state. He fights against the emperor for some years, with further political complexities still there under the surface, and there are threats to those under Ernst's care—specifically the city of Regensburg, which is under siege for a long time—but it is really the state he is fighting, and realizing the ultimate futility of this, he goes into exile, aided by his mother, who has been unable to effect a reconciliation. With a group of followers he escapes first to Hungary, the enemy kingdom of the Magyars (over whom the real Otto the Great had a significant victory), then to Byzantine Greece, where the Eastern emperor is referred to as *kunic*, king. That emperor, Nikephoros II Phokas (who ruled from 963 to 969), also had an uneasy relationship with Otto. From here Ernst sets sail, purportedly for Palestine in the first instance, and now we hear of his adventures among strange peoples in increasingly far-off lands. This central part of the work is framed by the first story.

The central—second—section is not unlike a *Bildungsroman*, a novel of education, in which Ernst accumulates experience as he gradually works his way (and this is unusual for a *Bildungsroman*) *back* to the status at which he actually started in the real world, ruler of a dukedom, although he may now be thought of as actually meriting what he was originally simply given. It has to be said that in spite of the (over)use by the poet of positive adjectives applied to Ernst, in the adventure section he is by no means always the ideal hero, especially in the earlier stages—most notably, as indicated, among the crane-headed people, from whom he tries to rescue the Indian princess. He and his friend and companion Wetzel are frankly immature, self-indulgent, and not very wise in their behavior. They do, however, gradually learn how to cope with adversity, how to help others, and how to serve.

Ernst also progresses geographically back from the unknown realms to more-familiar ones (albeit the geography is always a little eccentric), and thence to Germany. What he learns is how to occupy a proper position within a legitimate state, powerful but subordinate. After a period as a crusader he returns to do formal penance before the emperor and is reconciled. Since he is said to have brought back from his travels not only assorted exotic creatures but also the jewel known as "the orphan stone" that will become the central stone of the imperial crown, indeed itself the very symbol of the empire, his example is given a permanent and visible acknowledgment. The writer tells us that since anyone can see this stone in the crown jewels of the Holy Roman Empire, the story must be true.

The orphan stone, it may be noted, is no longer in the imperial crown of Charlemagne, the *Reichskrone* (which is kept in Vienna), but it was described in the thirteenth century as having been the color of red wine, so it was presumably a large ruby. It is unclear what happened to it, and it is not documented after the mid-fourteenth century. There is now a sapphire in the prominent position in the imperial crown. Even so, Ernst's discovery, as they pass through an underground river, of that imperial gemstone serves as a reminder of what these adventures of Ernst's are ultimately about, as well as providing a link between the two parts of the work, and incidentally underlining its supposed veracity.

The giants, pygmies, and people with cranes' heads or gigantic feet encountered by Ernst are medieval equivalents of the bug-eyed monsters of science fiction, and like quite a lot of science fiction, things always remain rooted in recognizable political contexts, with the adventures usually subordinated to a military-political point. Ernst's adventures are of course exciting, and the poet often points this up with words like "amazing" (*wunderlîch*), but as Ernst and his gradually dwindling band move farther away from the known world, and the people that they encounter become ever stranger, the travelers, and especially Ernst as the leader, require bravery and strategic ingenuity to survive.

Ernst takes service with the cyclops king of Arimaspi, helping him to defeat various even more outlandish enemies who have terrible weapons or special advantages. However odd they may look, closer consideration usually shows them to be principally very dangerous. The sciapods, for example, are known from other early writings, although here they have two feet like broad swan's feet, rather than just one large human foot. The Greek name means "shadow-foot" and so can be retained to translate *plathüeve*, "flatfeet," even if classically they were monopods. The writer says, of course, that they are *wunderlîch*, curious, and it may initially sound comical or even ludicrous when we are told that they can shelter from the rain by lying down with first one broad foot and then the other over them; similarly, the classical monopods are often depicted with their foot over their heads. But far more essentially—and this is the real point here—these creatures' feet can cover rough terrain just like tank tracks; they are never bothered by weather; and furthermore, they have fearsome weapons that fire what are presumably lethal bolts (*geschôz freislich*), so that the tank analogy is not too far-fetched. For defeating them, Ernst earns another dukedom from the king, and he then rewards his warriors, taking up the place in the kingdom of the Arimaspi, which he had once held in the empire. Duke Ernst once more, he returns home via the Holy Land as a penitent (a role adopted also by the historical Liudolf of Swabia in Otto's time), and the emperor pardons him, something engineered by the empress with the support of the princes.

There are several distinct narrative models visible as the whole work unfolds. If the framework is political and (loosely) historical, the adventure section contains elements of the suspense story, of quasi-chivalric romance, of straightforward battle-narrative, and of crusading Christianity, sometimes not entirely successfully integrated. An example is provided by Ernst's first major experience in the unknown world, when he finds himself in a land called Grippia, which is occupied by the crane-headed people. Their city is empty when he arrives, providing for mystery, and there is suspense when, in a spirit of pure adventure, he and his companion, Wetzel, go back without their men. The crane-headed people have returned with the captured princess from India, whom Ernst and Wetzel determine to rescue. This service to a beautiful lady (she is repeatedly thus designated, but never really described) fails, and she dies. The story now becomes one of battle as the two warriors fight their way out, to be rescued in the nick of time by the arrival of their shipmates as reinforcements. Just before they can regain their ship, however, they are attacked again, and the story becomes abruptly one of Christians versus pagans in the spirit of the *Chanson de Roland*, which famously asserted that Christians are right and pagans are wrong. Ernst's men are suddenly referred to as "the Christians," and now they are fighting for a share in the joys of heaven, rather than just for honor and renown. Those who get away are then referred to as *die edelen pilgerîne*, the noble pilgrims, and their Christianity and willingness to do penance for their sins are stressed from then on until they reach Jerusalem.

Historically this work (which overlaps to a small extent with Konrad's novella) reflects to a degree an incident in the life of the genuine Otto I, the Saxon emperor of the Holy Roman Empire (962–73), known as Otto the Great, who was in 953 in dispute with his son Liudolf, duke of Swabia, which led to war and eventually to a siege of Regensburg. This is probably the basis for the story, but the name Ernst and some other points have been taken over from a later Duke Ernst of Swabia, who was in conflict with his stepfather, another rather later emperor, Konrad II (1027–39). Otto the Great was first married to the Anglo-Saxon princess Edgitha (Edith, here called Ottegebe), and thereafter to Adelheid (Adelaide) of Burgundy. Adelaide's first husband had sought help from Liudolf of Swabia in a conflict that set Liudolf against his uncle, Henry of Bavaria, so that distorted echoes of all these events may be heard in the story. The duchies of Bavaria and of Swabia were among the five most important duchies of the Holy Roman Empire.

The story of Ernst was very well known in a wide variety of versions in German and Latin from the twelfth to the fifteenth century and indeed beyond (though not all versions depend on our poem) and was echoed in Czech and Icelandic as well, but the earliest full text, known in German studies as *Herzog Ernst B*, is translated here. It represents a revision of an earlier A-text, of which we have some fragments, and which was composed probably toward the end of the twelfth and revised in the early thirteenth century, during the high period of Middle High German literature. Other versions include a ballad-style text from the end of the Middle Ages, and also a prose chapbook; different versions were rediscovered and taken up again in the nineteenth century by the German Romantics and adapted in various forms, and many of the texts have been edited separately. It is of particular interest that the story was used as a satire in the former German Democratic Republic by the dramatist Peter Hacks (1928–2003) in his play *Das Volksbuch von Herzog Ernst, oder: Der Held und sein Gefolge* (1961; first performed, 1967). Hacks gives us an emperor's-eye-view of the feudal system that is worth citing because it is witty and also provides another satirical-political perspective. For the medieval writer, of course, these were the realities of a system that had to be shown to work, whatever the overall social implications of the feudal system might be in historical terms. For all that, Hacks's imagining of the emperor's view of life, politics, and everything else might not be restricted to a twelfth-century ruler and is certainly double edged. Hacks's Emperor Otto sums up the whole system and his position in it this way:

> Truly, my lords, the thing that makes our age the very flower of all ages is the notion of ongoing subordination, or the concept of *ordo*, as my dear brother likes to put it. Look, right at the top there is me. Then, next in line are the dukes and earls, and my relatives, the bishops. These pass on their authority in turn to the barons and the monasteries. And then come the loyal knights and the yeomen citizens, whom I greatly cherish. Then the free farmers, who, if I am not mistaken, provide useful bread and nice little eggs for us, then the villeins and then the serfs. And the women—if you will permit me to mention them in this context—they too receive a certain kind of fief from us. (My translation; details of edition below)

A comical-obscene rejoinder to this last remark from the bishop of Cologne, his brother, saying that they use their staffs of office on a nightly basis to give something to the women, is not well received by the emperor.

* * *

The standard edition of *Herzog Ernst B* is that by Karl Bartsch (Vienna: Braumüller, 1869; repr. Hildesheim, Olms, 1969). Bartsch's text is also available along with a modern German version, notes, and a bibliography by Bernhard Sowinski (Stuttgart: Reclam, 1970). There is also a new edition by Mathias Herweg, *Herzog Ernst* (Stuttgart: Reclam, 2019). The work has been translated into English prose by J. W. Thomas and Carolyn Dussère as *The Legend of Duke Ernst* (Lincoln: University of Nebraska Press, 1979). There is a wealth of secondary literature, and material continues to appear, especially in German, such as Gerd Althoff, *Brüchige Helden—brüchiges Erzählen* (Göttingen: de Gruyter, 2017), and smaller specific studies such as Rasma Lazda-Cazera, "Hybridity and Liminality in *Herzog Ernst B*," *Daphnis* 33 (2004): 79–96, on the Grippia episode. There is a good earlier introduction in English by David Blamires, *Herzog Ernst and the Otherworld Voyage* (Manchester: Manchester University Press, 1979). I have discussed the text and also that by Konrad in my *The Germanic Hero: Politics and Pragmatism in Early Medieval Poetry* (London: Hambledon, 1996). Peter Hacks's readable play *Das Volksbuch von Herzog Ernst, oder: Der Held und sein Gefolge* is in his *Stücke* (Leipzig: Reclam, 1978), 5–65. For comments on the idea of the "minstrel epic," see my note (on a study by Sarah Bowden) "Laying the Ghost of the 'Spielmannsepos,'" *Medium Aevum* 85 (2016): 323–27. A forty-five-minute cartoon film was made by Lutz Dammbeck in 1993. There are editions of other medieval versions and of nineteenth-century adaptations.

Konrad von Würzburg, *Henry of Kempten*

The second text, a shorter and in many ways simpler work, is the tale of Henry of Kempten, a minor nobleman much farther down the echelons of the feudal system than Ernst but still part of it. Caught up (again fairly honorably) in a sequence of what look like trivial events but escalate, logically and inexorably, the knight Henry finds himself holding a knife to the throat of the emperor, Otto, in front of the political worthies of the empire and very nearly brings the entire state down around him. He stops short of doing so, but as happens to Ernst in the first text, the emperor banishes him. When he is later forced by his feudal obligations to fight alongside the emperor against an outside enemy, fate places him in a position where he saves—in very unusual circumstances—the life of that same emperor he once nearly killed. He is forgiven, and has had some time to learn his lesson in any case, but the moral, and hence the message of this work in political terms (similarly to *Duke Ernst*), is that any political system is fragile, and even apparently small events can trigger an escalation.

Konrad von Würzburg was born in the city by whose name he is known sometime between 1220 and 1235 and died in Basel on August 31, 1287. He was a prolific and capable German poet writing in the second half of the thirteenth century. He was not a nobleman. His works vary considerably in scope and genre (including history and hagiography) and are often marked by what look like very conservative attitudes. He was capable of high-flown style, but he is perhaps at his most impressive in his short narrative pieces, works of precision of which the text provided here is one example. The text bears no title, and Konrad refers to it simply as *diz maere*, "this tale." It has been referred to variously as *Otto mit dem Bart*, "Bearded Otto," "Otto Red-Beard," and, as titled here, *Heinrich von Kempten*, "Henry of Kempten." Either Otto or Henry would do as the title character, since these are the two main figures, but the empire itself is really the principal theme. The work was written in the 1260s or 1270s for an ecclesiastical patron called Berthold von Tiersberg and is in 770 lines of rhymed couplets.

The events of the story start off calmly. Konrad's opening is brief but nevertheless presents a very full picture of the state at the imperial Easter (and hence supposedly peaceful) celebration, where we are given a positively cinematic representative picture of the entire feudal society. At this celebration a young boy, who is as it happens a powerful duke's son, unthinkingly breaks off a piece of bread before he is supposed to; the emperor's steward overdoes his chastisement of the boy and draws blood. Henry, the boy's guardian, who is feudally obliged to protect the boy, kills the steward (in a most unchivalric manner: with a club). The emperor demands the killer's death, and in an attempt to save his own life, since he just been summarily condemned by the ill-tempered Otto "by my beard," Henry holds a knife to the emperor's throat. Complete chaos could ensue: if the emperor were killed, there would be a bloodbath and a civil war. In spite of the regular nods to courtly or chivalric behavior, this story is from the start balanced on the edge of chaos, and although it purports to be about the supposed lack of nobility and courtly decency in the narrator's day, a *laudatio temporis acti*, it is really about the ease with which violence can escalate and about the precarious nature of politics in an armed society (which includes our present-day society). This is no medieval romance; there is no quest, no knight-errantry, and there are indeed no ladies mentioned at all. The emperor is characterized as hot-tempered and unpleasant, while the protagonist, Henry of Kempten, is an excellent knight. We need not always take these comments too seriously (Konrad also plays with us by referring from time to time to his "source"); the emperor does, however, learn to a small extent to moderate his behavior, and Henry also learns a lesson over a period of years. Above all, however, the emperor is the emperor, the symbol of the state, the one element, unpleasant or not, that holds the state together.

When Henry grabs the emperor by his famous red beard, the imperial crown is symbolically already on the floor. This might lead to civil war and disputed succession, and a great many dead. In fact, it does not; the emperor waves his supporters back so as to save his own life. However trivial the beginning, it is hard to overestimate the seriousness of the situation now arrived at. Henry spares the emperor but is banished under pain of death from the emperor's sight. Henry had no choice but to fight for his life (we might note that he is clearly carrying a dagger, too, another unchivalric weapon), and the supposedly formal and peaceful gathering of all the estates has been seriously disrupted. Society has an inbuilt propensity to chaos, especially when assisted by the impetuousness of youth and the arrogance of age.

Years later—after he has settled down and led an exemplary life—Henry finds himself summoned to join the emperor's forces. (That he answers the call is not without a certain amount of self-interest, in that he might otherwise lose his estates.) Once again, then, his feudal duty (and the direct threat to his fiefs) requires that he accompany the prince-abbot of Kempten to fight in an imperial army during a siege in Italy. While taking a bath, he sees the emperor ride into an ambush and be attacked, and, in spite of his personal feelings toward Otto, he lays hands on a shield and sword and fights off the attack, naked as he stands. For this affirmation of loyalty he is pardoned by the emperor. The unusual nature of this event—what would later in German writings about the novella form be called "the logically developed but completely novel happening"—is also symbolic: Henry is reduced to nakedness apart from his shield and sword and can rely only on these appropriate weapons (in contrast to the earlier club and the dagger) and his innate loyalty. He is compelled by the society of which he is part, and in which he has himself accepted benefits, to carry out in return for his benefits any duties that his overlord, the abbot, requires, however reluctant he might be to do so. Indeed, when his inner nobility makes him defend the threatened emperor and therefore the stability of the state, he is in effect defending himself, because he is part of it. Not that the emperor is himself entirely worthy, except as an embodiment of the state itself; he is unpleasant and prone to condemning without trial and to swearing by his beard—hardly a legal oath. It is not exactly a measure of the emperor's glory that he has to be rescued by a single naked warrior when he has ridden straight into an ambush, although after the rescue his followers apply the word *maere*, glorious, to him.

Elements within the system might be bad, but the system itself has to be regarded as sound. Henry has acted bravely not just in fighting but in fulfilling his feudal duties. The emperor has learned to show generosity. To be sure, when the reconciliation occurs, Henry says once again that he came on the campaign because otherwise he would have forfeited his own feudal holdings from the abbot, and in the last analysis Henry's loyalty is, like that of Ernst, not just to the feudal lords above him (the abbot, the emperor) but to the whole political system. Konrad is indeed conservative insofar as he expresses in his works regret about the change in mores and the decline of chivalric virtues; but this is no blimpish reluctance to come to terms with the changing times, nor does Konrad glorify the good old days as such. Failure to keep to proven and decent values is always potentially disastrous, and here the noble behavior that he claims is declining just about manages to keep in balance the very political stability that the same warrior nearly wrecked in the first place. The broader picture is more worrying than the perceived deficiencies, which are always possible, whether in the ruler or in the subordinate.

The most difficult line to translate in the work comes when Henry has his dagger at the emperor's throat. The imperial crown has already fallen and is lying on the ground, and Henry says, "ich stiche im ab den weisen," "I'll cut from him the great jewel." The jewel is referred to in the text as the orphan (*weise*) and is the single great gemstone, the orphan stone, the ruby that once sat at the center of the imperial crown. The threat of removing the gemstone at the center of the crown, which played a part in *Duke Ernst* and which is used elsewhere in medieval German as a kind of shorthand, a metonym for the whole imperial crown and thus for the empire itself, implies that Henry will, if forced, destroy the empire. The threat to the imperial crown is as symbolic as, perhaps, an attack on the British Houses of Parliament in the seventeenth century or on the US Capitol in more recent times.

Konrad von Würzburg was for some time classed somewhat dismissively as an epigone, a latecomer, and indeed he pretends to be looking back to the age of courtly nobility. In fact, he is looking back here to the age of Ottonian rule, three centuries earlier in the prechivalric tenth century, and his narrative is set in an even more distorted version of tenth-century history than that in *Duke Ernst*. Once again, the sometimes-tenuous historical links need not concern us unduly, even though Konrad claims slyly to have read the story, as if it were some kind of a chronicle.

In the later part of the tenth century, the Holy Roman Empire, which had been ruled by the Saxon Otto I, the Great (962–73), was less stable after his reign, and the political situation in the various lands that composed the empire was often precarious. Otto the Great was succeeded by his son, Otto II (973–83), who was known as Rufus, meaning "the Red," and in that respect, at least, offers a parallel with Konrad's Otto (albeit the best-known red-bearded emperor is the rather later Frederick Barbarossa in the twelfth century). Some early images have Otto II bearded, but many do not. It is hard to tell on his coins, but even on these there seems to be no sign of a long and graspable beard. His ten-year reign as emperor is also, incidentally, not long enough for the events of the story, let alone for such a well-established beard. Otto II did, however, mount a campaign in Italy in 981–82 that was not always successful (he had to escape from the Battle of Stilo in July 982), so that this, too, may be echoed in Konrad's work. Otto II died suddenly when still only in his late twenties and was technically succeeded by his only son, who was a child at the time. The son eventually ruled as Otto III from 996 to 1002 following a period of (contested) government by various regents and would-be regents after the death of his father. These included his older second cousin, Henry of Bavaria, who—again eventually and after a certain amount of chaos—did become the next emperor after the death of Otto III at twenty-one, ruling as Henry II from 1014 to 1024 and dying without an heir, the last of the dynasty. He was succeeded by Konrad II, to whom reference has already been made. There may also be echoes in the work of later historical events in the Holy Roman Empire, such as the disputed succession to the imperial throne at the beginning of the thirteenth century. The murder of Philip of Swabia, the Hohenstaufen claimant, took place at Bamberg in 1208, although in this case it *ended* (albeit temporarily) the civil war between the great families of Welf and Hohenstaufen. Konrad seems to think of the past in some respects as a golden age; but this is a limited view: if Philip's murder is reflected in Otto's close encounter with death, then that was at least in Konrad's own century, one that in its latter part and his own lifetime saw the Great Interregnum (1250–73) in the Holy Roman Empire and political chaos once again until the start of Habsburg rule in 1282.

Kempten in Swabia (Bavaria, not far from Lake Constance) had an imperial monastery founded by the wife of Charlemagne in 773, which was in the charge of an imperially appointed prince-abbot, who would have been obliged to provide troops for the emperor from his own feudal lands if called upon to do so. The duke of Swabia himself—a personage relevant to both *Duke Ernst* and *Henry of Kempten*—was one of the most important nobles of the empire, and the office was held from the end of the eleventh century by the Hohenstaufen family.

*   *   *

The standard edition of the Middle High German text is that edited by Edward Schröder, *Kleinere Dichtungen Konrads von Würzburg,* vol. 1, 8th ed. (Dublin and Zurich: Weidmann, 1967), with an afterword by Ludwig Wolff. There is a convenient edition (based on Schröder) with a modern German translation in *Konrad von Würzburg,* translated by Heinz Rölleke (Stuttgart: Reclam, 1968), with a later edition by Lydia Miklautsch, *Konrad von Würzburg: Das Hermaere und andere Verserzählungen* (Stuttgart: Reclam, 2028), and an English translation in J. W. Thomas, *The Best Novellas of Medieval Germany* (Columbia, SC: Camden House, 1984), 55–61. There is an edition with a prose translation and notes by Alan V. Murray, "The Wicked Emperor and the Knight in the Bathtub," *Leeds Medieval Studies* 1 (2021): 59–89 (also available online). On Konrad's text, see (as noted above) my *The Germanic Hero,* and there is a more recent study on the violence (and on the sources) by Gustavo Fernández Riva, "Critic of Courtliness in Konrad von Würzburg's *Heinrich von Kempten,*" *Viator* 49 (2018): 187–98. The theme of social disruption is addressed by Monika Schausten, "Beim Bart des Kaisers: Soziales Chaos und poetische Ordnung in Konrads von Würzburg *Heinrich von Kempten,*" in *Erzählte Ordnungen— Ordnungen des Erzählens,* ed. Daniela Fuhrmann and Pia Selmayr (Berlin: de Gruyter, 2021), 230–49.

Heinrich (*der glîchezâre*), Reynard the Fox

This work in its original form predates that by Konrad, but its grim conclusion is such that it is better placed last in the sequence, since this time the legitimate ruler actually *does* lose his life, and to a scoundrel. The actors are animals, but the behavior is (mostly) human. We know very little about the author, and even his name, which is frequently given as Heinrich *der glîchezâre*, the Middle High German tag meaning "hypocrite," is unclear and can also just be translated as "fabulist" or "storyteller." But it is a convenient enough tag to help separate this writer from numerous other Heinrichs. He seems to have come from Alsace, wrote at the end of the twelfth century, and has been described as "a minstrel," which means not much more than "a writer." *Reinhart Fuchs,* or *Reynard the Fox,* is the title given at the head of the text, which in the modern standard edition has 2,266 lines in rhymed couplets. The style is fairly simple, and the work can be fitted into a familiar literary genre. It is—on the surface anyway—an animal fable, using the technique, which goes back to Aesop and is known from Geoffrey Chaucer, Jean de La Fontaine, and many others, of tales where animals have human characteristics (while remaining animals) and therefore can make distanced points about human life. It is a tradition that in English alone not only includes Chaucer's *Canterbury Tales* (1387–1400)—whose highly articulate fowls in "The Nun's Priest's Tale" quote classical authors but then behave in more appropriately gallinaceous fashion, reminding us that they are, indeed, hens and a rooster—but also George Orwell, who famously merges the pigs and the men at the end of *Animal Farm* (1945).

At the center are the various (mis)adventures of the titular fox. They make up a sequence of separate short episodes, in the earliest of which (some of them very familiar as independent fables) he is less than successful. Already in the early stages his innate malice is signaled, however; he plans not just to steal the cheese from the crow but also, gratuitously, to kill the bird, and he wants to send Tibert the cat into a trap. Perhaps, too, his failures in these early incidents shape his later approach to life, since in the later anecdotes he is revealed increasingly not just as a trickster (the fox is part of the broad narrative trickster tradition) but also as a thief, a rapist, and a murderer. The series of episodes between the fox and the wolf—brain against brawn—form a middle section to the work. The last part (which comes a little while after a hiatus in the text—there is a part missing) has the fox attacking the wolf and others ever more viciously and gradually assuming a major role in the kingdom of the beasts ruled by the lion, who at one point, like Emperor Otto, swears "by my beard." Reynard poses as court physician, and most of the other animals, large or small and whether they have helped him or not, are in rapid succession humiliated or even killed. Bruin the bear seems to survive being skinned, but poor Pinte, Chantecler's wife and the mother of a chicken killed by Reynard but beatified after occasioning a miracle, ends up as a hot meal for the fox. After all this vengeful malice Reynard is in a position at the end to murder—completely gratuitously— the gullible and not very bright lion king. What did you expect? asks the narrator. There is entertainment and comedy in some of the episodes (the beatification of the chicken is a case in point), and there is a mixture of human and animal settings for the individual episodes, but the all-too-human overall behavior attributed to the fox as political animal in a quite literal sense is, in its cumulative effect, very far from comic.

The work is part of a ramified literary tradition revolving around Reynard (Reginhart, Reinardus, Renart, Reinhart, Rein[e]ke, Reynaerde) the Fox. There are foxes in Aesop, but the earliest relevant medieval text is in Latin, and the tradition is especially well developed in French (which took over his Germanic name as the word for a fox) in the different versions of the *Roman de Renart*. Heinrich's version is an early spin-off from this literary branch, although its oldest manuscript in fact predates the manuscripts of the surviving French texts. There are Low German/Dutch parallels, and the tradition came via Dutch into English with the help of the printer William Caxton in 1481, although the crafty fox, with a different name, appears already in memorable form in Chaucer's "Nun's Priest's Tale."

Johann Wolfgang von Goethe's version (1794) also derives ultimately from the Dutch text, and there are plenty of other post-medieval versions or adaptations. The manuscript transmission of Heinrich's version is equally complicated. There is an early incomplete text in one manuscript from the end of the twelfth century, but it survives in full (except for the gap) in a later reworking, which seems to be a closely related but linguistically updated text, in two fourteenth-century manuscripts, of which that in Heidelberg (manuscript Cpg 341, known as P) is the one taken as a basis for the present translation.

* * *

The standard edition, in the *Altdeutsche Textbibliothek*, is *Das mittelhochdeutsche Gedicht vom Fuchs Reinhart*, ed. Georg Baesecke, 2nd ed., ed. Ingeborg Schröbler (Halle/Saale: Niemeyer, 1952). Once more there is a convenient edition based on this in the ever-useful Reclam collection, again with a modern German translation, valuable notes, and a clear presentation of the relationship of the surviving manuscripts: Karl-Heinz Göttert, *Heinrich der Glîchezâre, Reinhart Fuchs* (Stuttgart: Reclam, 1974). There is an English translation by J. W. Thomas in *German Medieval Tales*, ed. Francis G. Gentry (New York: Continuum, 2002), 84–113. The work was for some time examined less frequently than many other medieval German texts, but there is an important study by Ute Schwab, *Zur Datierung und Interpretation des Reinhart Fuchs* (Naples: AION, 1967; repr. 2010), and a brief and to-the-point assessment in the literary history by Karl Bertau, *Deutsche Literatur in europäischen Mittelalter*, vol. 1 (Munich: Beck, 1972), 717–23. On the earliest tradition, see Jan M. Ziolkowski, *Talking Animals: Medieval Latin Beast Poetry 750–1150* (Philadelphia: University of Pennsylvania Press, 1993), and on the technicalities of law, Sigrid Widmaier, *Das Recht im "Reinhart Fuchs"* (Berlin: de Gruyter, 1993). There is a useful paper by Jean-Marc

Pastré, "Morals, Justice and Geopolitics in the *Reinhart Fuchs* of the Alsatian Heinrich der Glichezaere," in *Reynard the Fox: Social Engagement and Cultural Metamorphoses in the Beast Epic*, ed. Kenneth Varty (New York: Berghahn, 2000), 37–54. More-recent interest in the work is evidenced by two *Beihefte* (supplements) to the journal *Germanisch-Romanische Monatsschrift*: Marion Darilek, *Füchsische Desintegration: Studien zum "Reinhart Fuchs"* (Heidelberg: Winter, 2020), and Jan Glück, *Animal homificans* (Heidelberg: Winter, 2021). Literature on Reynard as such is predictably extensive, but to select one book in English only: Kenneth Varty, *Reynard the Fox: A Study of the Fox in Medieval English Art* (Leicester: Leicester University Press, 1967), is both instructive and entertaining.

Translating the Texts

The three works translated here are all good narratives, demonstrating a wide range of storytelling techniques and offering entertainment as well as providing food for thought, which justifies their presentation as a group. As far as form goes, all three works are in verse, specifically in rhymed couplets, which was customary for narratives at a time when stories were recited and listened to. A modern English translation into that form would run the permanent risk, however, of coming close to doggerel. The normal form for the presentation of narratives nowadays is plain prose, which is most often read silently by the individual, and accordingly these works have been translated into prose. One inescapable problem, however, is that the need for rather a lot of repeated rhymes in the originals limits the vocabulary available to the medieval writer—and hence the translator—given the convenience of groups like *guot/muot/tuot* (good/spirit/does) and many others. Trying to render the original in a rhymed translation would make things even more difficult, and as a further and quite specific argument against attempting to imitate the rhymed couplets, there is in *Duke Ernst* a fairly long passage when the hero and a companion inspect and take advantage of an apparently empty but very well-appointed citadel, the furnishings and fittings of which are described in enormous detail. It is a delaying passage deliberately intended to build up suspense (which makes it an ancestor of the tale of Goldilocks and the Three Bears), but the prospect of rendering lengthy descriptions of medieval bedspreads and hot-and-cold plumbing (however spectacular) into rhymed verse would be very daunting indeed.

Translating into prose does, of course, give a certain license for variation, but the possibilities are still restricted by the original, which uses not only repeated rhymes but regularly reiterated quasi-formulaic designations, in which warriors are almost always *edel*, noble, with only a small selection of other attributive adjectives, including the all-purpose *guot*, good, and indeed *küene*, bold. Sometimes the only answer is simply to leave the descriptors out where there is a danger otherwise of an overload of nobility. Furthermore, are they knights? Warriors? Heroes? Thanes? It is a separate difficulty to avoid archaizing. Even in *Reynard the Fox* the main character's much-repeated chief attribute, cunning (*list*), needs to be varied from time to time.

I have also taken a few liberties with names and titles in *Duke Ernst*, using modern English equivalents of familiar names for the most part but leaving Ernst, for fear of unconsciously invoking Oscar Wilde. For titles, the jealous Henry of the Rhine and Ernst's friend Wetzel both have the title *Graf*; the former is actually a *Pfalzgraf*, but while I have afforded him the usual version of what is in fact an elevated title without a real equivalent, "count palatine," I have given to Wetzel the English (subducal) title of earl, thus keeping the two men nominally as well as morally apart. I have also added full names from time to time to make clear exactly who is meant at any given point.

In translating *Reinhart Fuchs* I have used the name Reynard as the most familiar form for the central character, and other animals have names that recur in varying forms within the tradition, such as Chantecler the cockerel (though the hen's name is Pinte here, rather than Pertelot or Partlet), Isengrim the wolf (whose wife is usually Hirsent, though it varies a little here), or Grimbard the badger (here Krimel), or Bruin the bear. I have tried to use the most familiar form. The cat, here called Diepreht, is in English versions usually Tibert, which I have used, since many cats are to this day called Tibby (or variations thereof). Tybalt, Romeo's rival in Shakespeare's play, has a related name and is thus called "the prince of cats," but borrowing that name might be confusing. There is a small problem with the lion, who in the French tradition is called Noble. Heinrich calls him Vrevil, which looks like the modern German noun *Frevel*, meaning "outrage." In Middle High German, however, the word as an adjective means "brave," "bold," and in that sense "noble," although it could also have a quite separate negative meaning. Here it seems to be a translation of the French, and to avoid confusion I have retained Noble. Other beasts are unnamed, or their names are not familiar. Dizelin is technically (and unusually) a raven in this version, but in most versions of Reynard's failed theft of the cheese, from Aesop to La Fontaine, the bird is a crow, which is what I have made him. He seems not to have a fixed name. Reynard also regularly refers to the other birds and beasts when he is trying to trick them as if they were relatives—cousins or nephews—which sounds odd in English even in an anthropomorphic context, so I have, in the interests of greater zoological plausibility, usually let him address them simply as his friends; an exception is possible with the wolf, even if the lynx, tomcat, and badger remain somewhat more dubious relatives. *Pate*, the title Reynard gives the wolf, means "godfather" or "sponsor," so I have usually rendered it as "patron" to try and indicate the relationship as implied by the fox.

Human names and designations can also pose problems, and I have had to resort, for example, to mild archaism for the farmer and his wife plagued by Reynard. The actual names vary in the text, so I have simply made them consistent, but the wife is termed *baba, babe*, "old woman," in Middle High German. The best-known parallel for this word is probably the name of the fearsome Slavic witch Baba Yaga. Göttert's modern German translation has "*Mütterchen*," but while "old mother" might be a possible equivalent (as in Old Mother Hubbard), or even "granny" (the relationship word survives as *bobe* in modern Yiddish), I have gone back to the title "Gammer," as in *Gammer Gurton's Needle*. One name that has defeated everyone, however, is that of an enigmatic character who is neither animal nor human. Kunin (the spelling varies even in the text) appears to be a malicious elf, a demon, or a wood-spirit of some kind. I have gone for "goblin." Names of actual historical figures (like Walther of Horburg) have to be left as they are, even if they are no longer familiar; the secondary literature mentioned, especially that by Schwab, is helpful in explaining such personal and place names and the (very few) contemporary allusions.

I have, finally, added not just paragraph breaks but also ad hoc chapter divisions and headings for *Duke Ernst* and for *Reynard the Fox*. These are not in the originals. Konrad's novella is complete, concise, and coherent in itself and needs no subdivisions. An indication of the line numbers of all three works is, however, provided in square brackets at the ends of appropriate sections of the narrative.

DUKE ERNST

CHAPTER 1

THE YOUNG NOBLEMAN

Here begins the story of a brave warrior and his amazing adventures. It is well worth paying attention and giving it due consideration, because it is a really inspiring tale of boldness and bravery. After all, there are plenty of stay-at-home types whose secret sorrow it is that they never dared to try out the hard but adventurous life of a warrior for themselves. They are the losers in this, as far as noble behavior is concerned, because they never suffered these hardships and, indeed, kept well clear of them, simply because that is the sort of people they are. People like that are forever saying that the kind of story I'm going to tell is all a pack of lies, and they make every effort to belittle and even to suppress tales like this, just as if they actually *were* nothing but lies. But people like that are really not worth bothering about. Decent honest warriors, on the other hand, don't take the slightest notice of their put-downs. They themselves will set out on hazardous journeys in strange lands to prove what they are, and will suffer the bad times with the good out there among the most outlandish peoples. They, of course, would not cast doubt on adventure stories of this kind, because they have themselves experienced that kind of thing. I'm telling you all this now so that you will pay proper attention to the story I am about to tell you, and because I have no intention of playing down the sufferings and hardships that had to be faced by Duke Ernst when he was driven out of Bavaria. [1–37]

* * *

It is well documented that Ernst, our hero, once ruled as duke of Bavaria, and took admirable care of both the poor and the rich in his lands, so that in all his deeds he was held in considerable esteem. The young man had ruled highly competently over the inheritance that his father had left him, until an emperor—with the full power of the empire behind him—drove him out and put such fear into many of Ernst's followers that they deserted him. He went into (an entirely honorable) exile, taking with him many brave warriors, all of whom risked life and limb at his side and were loyal to him even to death. He suffered a great many hardships, but he overcame all adversities bravely, because he was a hero to the core.

I need to explain how it came about that this young nobleman came into such damaging conflict with the power of the state. It appears that he was still just a child when his father died, but his father left him the lands and also a retinue of nobles who were prepared to serve him, and they brought him up—as indeed they should—and protected him from harm. His mother, a highly born lady named Adelaide, was both eminently respectable and widely respected. She had her son taught both Italian and Latin, and while he was still young, she sent him to Byzantium as part of his education. There he came into contact with scholars in all kinds of disciplines, and since he worked hard at everything, the lad soon became very highly regarded indeed.

That, then, is how this lively youngster spent his childhood years—getting to know foreign countries—and he established a reputation for himself in many of those kingdoms because he behaved so admirably in every respect when he was there. People often talked about him, and always favorably. He was a modest, honest, and generous young man, and because of that he gathered around himself a group of loyal friends who would stand by him when he needed them.

The young man established a reputation for decent and open behavior, and he made every effort to maintain it, something in which he succeeded. He really hated slander and deceitfulness. For the sake of his own reputation, and because it is a Christian thing to do, he was generous in sharing his riches. He was polite to his subordinates and vassals and afforded them all appropriate honors, something that meant that they supported him when he ran into trouble later on and remained under his command wherever he wanted them to go. Everyone stood by him and never left him as long as they lived, whether they were freeborn subjects or bondsmen.

And so the child grew up to be a man, to the age at which he knew it was time to bear arms himself. When he asked for all the appropriate arrangements to be made, this was soon done, and he was provided with a battle-charger, a riding horse, and a mail-coat. He was then knighted with great ceremony, along with another young nobleman, his liegeman, Earl Wetzel, a man of unflinching courage, as well as a number of other companions who had been brought up beside him in the ways of chivalry since they were children. Wetzel was therefore duty-bound to show faith and loyalty to him and never to abandon him whatever perils they had to face, and he did indeed stand bravely by him until the end of his days. The two men traveled together in a multitude of foreign countries, and they were never separated, however dangerous the situation was—until eventually death parted them.

After our noble hero had (together with the brave Earl Wetzel) formally been elevated to the status of a knight, he found himself a man of considerable power and influence. Nor did he disappoint anyone, and in all the German-speaking lands there was absolutely no one who could be considered his equal. He would travel through his lands accompanied by an impressive retinue of knights and squires, whom he treated extremely well, providing them with money and with equipment. His generosity ensured that he was well liked everywhere, and—ever mindful of his standing in the eyes of the world—he was never miserly with his silver or his gold. And so his men followed this exemplary prince with great loyalty, regardless of any dangers they had to face. [38–158]

Adelaide, the dowager duchess, was delighted that she had brought up her son so well that he was so widely and unreservedly praised—she, too, had great respect for the young warrior. As far as her own life was concerned, she always behaved with womanly dignity, and because of her reputation as a woman of great virtue she was courted by a number of important princes. Her intelligence and indeed her personal fortune meant that many a prince would have welcomed her as a wife. But at that time the noble lady had decided that she would never remarry and wanted to live out her days in the chaste and pure state of widowhood, something which was a matter of regret to the noblemen in question.

At that time, the Holy Roman Empire was in the hands of a powerful and mighty ruler named Otto, who had sovereignty over the lands of many princes in German- and Italian-speaking territories. Moreover, this same ruler had conquered the lands of the Wends and of the Frisians, and one could name a great number of others who had become subject to his rule. Surrounded by all his princes, Otto bore the imperial crown and was acknowledged to rule well; he protected the widows and orphans of his lands against all dangers, and his writ ran over a vast territory. He imposed the most effective stability that there has ever been or ever will be, both inside and outside the lands of the Saxons.

To the greater glory and honor of God this emperor founded a mighty archbishopric at Magdeburg—a city on the banks of the river Elbe that is now universally celebrated. This was much to the displeasure of the devil, since people now turned away from him and paid proper attention to their eternal souls, and the emperor had persuaded them to do so quite without the use of force. Magdeburg Cathedral was dedicated to Saint Maurice and his Companions, and of course to the greater glory of God, who had granted him a place among His saints. Otto endowed the cathedral with lands and men and augmented this with financial support, and for this he earned praise and honor in the eyes of the Lord.

The sovereign emperor had also established there, to the glory of God once more, a cathedral chapter, so that many voices are still raised every day to offer thanks to Our Lord for its founding. This powerful ruler well knew (I can assure you) how to bear himself in the most noble fashion. He was brave in battle and a doughty warrior, and the Holy Roman Empire was safe in his hands. He always behaved chivalrously toward rich and poor alike and was ready to give help to anyone who asked for it.

As a young man, the emperor had married a noblewoman who had since died, and whose body was buried (as was appropriate) in the cathedral. This most blessed lady—whose name was Edith—was by birth an Anglo-Saxon princess, and she bore Otto children as a fruitful vine. Always concerned to do God's will, when she died she was received into His realm and into the eternal joy, her soul now as blessed as was her earthly life. You may be interested to know that God permitted many miracles to happen for the sake of this lady, and these can be verified to this day. Anyone can see that God treated the noble lady with great mercy all the days of her life.

And so the emperor was now without a wife. He decided that he would be happy to remarry, someone suited to himself and also suitable as queen over the empire, and he called the princes together to make his thoughts known to them. "My dear friends," he said, "help me to act in a way that will please you and is appropriate, and find me a consort acceptable to yourselves. I shall be greatly indebted to you and shall reward you well, believe me."

When the princes heard this, they met in council and gave thought to how they could carry out their sovereign's wishes. They all agreed that they knew of no one who would be more suitable as a wife for him than the duchess Adelaide, a lady rightly praised above all other women. They knew nothing disadvantageous about her, and apparently all men of wisdom were in agreement on this point. "If the emperor could persuade her to be his wife, then that would be most acceptable to us all." If the emperor did consider her, they agreed that he would be able to place her with confidence on the imperial throne. She would, with her womanly virtues, be eminently suitable, and throughout her younger days she had always behaved in a decent and honorable manner.

They were all in accord, therefore. The princes now came to the great sovereign and told him all about the fine lady in question, about her nobility and virtue, her intelligence and the fact that she was still young, indeed, about her whole and wholly admirable cast of mind. They told him that she could with all honor become sovereign lady of the Holy Roman Empire, because she was quite without equal among all the ladies they knew of anywhere in German-speaking lands.

Once the emperor had heard all this, the advice seemed very good indeed, because the lady seemed to be so virtuous and noble. Accordingly, he waited no longer but wrote to her in his own hand—a skill he was eminently capable of—a letter containing sweet words as if directly from his mouth, the most tender that he could write. He chose an appropriate nobleman as an ambassador and sent him with the letter to Bavaria.

When this warrior arrived and presented the letter, the lady received him well and greeted him politely and amicably. The envoy explained with great dignity to the lady that the great ruler of the Holy Roman Empire had sent her an affectionate message, and that it was to be hoped that she would be kind enough to accede to the wishes of the emperor and of his princes, and that if she would grant this imperial wish she would forever be held in the highest esteem.

The duchess reacted with appropriate courtesy. She bowed as she took the letter and said, "I shall, as is my duty, be obedient to the wishes and needs of the state." Then the noble lady sent word to have her chaplain brought to her so that he could read her everything that was in the letter. This is what it said:

> Most noble duchess, this is a letter from the very hand of the sovereign ruler of the empire, who asks that you, as someone most virtuous and well brought up, should take careful account of its content. The emperor's counselors have told him much about your goodness, and he asks that you should turn your affection and your love toward him. For I shall make you the sovereign lady of the entire Holy Roman Empire, so that no other woman in the world would be your equal, and your lovely presence would become ever more greatly admired. Most worthy lady, all the princes, dukes, and earls of my empire would be yours to command, and you, most noble and admirable lady, would enjoy enormous esteem. I have heard a great deal about your virtues and ask you, my dear lady, not to be angry, but to grant to me and my princes the wish that I should be your husband. Then you shall want for nothing, as long as you shall live. I shall confer upon you the powers to do a great many things, and there will be much for you to enjoy, just as you wish. Those who at present count themselves your equals in rank will be subordinate to you, since you will be their queen.

When the noble lady had heard the contents of the letter and listened to what the imperial messenger had to say, she gave thanks to God in her heart and soul for the exalted honor that He had conferred upon her, and her spirit asked for His grace.

She then sent for her son and asked for him to come and hear about this imperial message. As was right and proper, she wanted his advice on this, and the young man soon presented himself in his mother's apartments. The duchess told him at once about the offer that had been made to her, and he was delighted to hear it. "It makes me very proud, too," he said, "and you should certainly not refuse, since he thinks so highly of you that he wants you as his wife. We can all rejoice with you, since you have been chosen by all the princes to be their sovereign lady. There is no need for any reflection on the matter. I can advise you in all loyalty that you should willingly accept his proposal." That was the young warrior's good advice.

When the lady heard that her son thought the proposal acceptable and advised her to agree, she sent the envoy back with a message to the emperor and all the court that she would gladly do all that he asked. The imperial messenger then returned happily, the noble lord in question riding hard day and night with hardly a rest until he reached the great emperor and at once reported to his lord what had been said. He was, of course, welcomed back and praised by the whole imperial court for having completed his mission so well in the name of the empire, and he received their grateful thanks. [159–448]

The most noble emperor was delighted with the response of the beautiful duchess, and his inner circle were all equally pleased with the news. Accordingly, on the command of the emperor, great preparations were now made, day and night, for a wedding in the imperial city of Mainz in six weeks' time. Meanwhile, he and his immediate court set off happily to Bavaria and his bride. A great throng of noble knights were present when Duchess Adelaide was betrothed to the ruler of the empire. The emperor and his court were all clearly delighted. When they set off to conduct the lady back, large numbers of bold warriors and happy shield-bearing knights accompanied her on her way. Great crowds thronged the streets so that sometimes they almost blocked the way on the long journey until they reached the city of Mainz.

When they had crossed the Rhine, they settled in a large and well-appointed camp that had been set up on the grass in the meadows on the edge of the city where the wedding was to take place. All kinds of entertainments were provided in celebration of the emperor's nuptials. You could hear the people singing, whooping, and shouting, and music from all kinds of stringed instruments, as well as all the usual fun and games you get at a wedding. Everyone, rich and poor alike, was in good spirits, and no finer celebration has been seen before or since in the entire Holy Roman Empire, something for which its great sovereign was acclaimed everywhere. He gave gifts to his warriors—expensive fabrics, fully equipped pack animals, silver, gold—and his aristocrats were all richly rewarded as well. It would be difficult to do justice to the extent of all these gifts and the pleasure they gave. There were plenty of itinerant musicians and minstrels there, too, and they—to their great delight—were also given expensive gifts.

Once the wedding had been celebrated, the princes, dukes, and earls, as well as a number of provosts and bishops, all presented themselves one by one to the emperor to take their leave, and the great court celebration broke up. All the individual warriors loyal to the crown now went happily on their way. The emperor and his beautiful wife then set out, accompanied by a large number of his men, to the palace he had decided upon as a residence. The noble queen was a great joy to him, and he treated her with enormous honor because of the love she bore for him. This beautiful and loving lady was dearer to him than any material goods, and he was always courteous and affectionate toward her. Nor did she ever for any reason cause him any distress, and her womanly graces ensured that she was always in his favor. Indeed, if he was ever upset by something that had happened, she had the happy ability to smooth things over for him. She treated him with so much love that he would forget his troubles because of her. They made a very good couple.

The emperor and the empress really loved each other and lived together for a long while without anything to disturb their contentment, because nowhere in their wider families was there any sign of a problem. How could things have been better? They lived in harmony, and at the same time the Holy Roman Empire enjoyed a time of peace and unsullied standing in the world, the like of which it had not known before. [449–557]

The emperor sent envoys to Duke Ernst, to whom he was very favorably inclined—his love for the duke's mother meant that he felt warmly about her son. The emperor offered love and friendship to the noble warrior, just as a powerful overlord should treat one of his vassals, and invited him cordially to come and visit the empress, his mother.

The duke agreed and took with him a fine retinue of his own men when he went to his sovereign's court. The emperor received the warrior courteously, as did the duke's mother, who was happy to see him. They gave the bold nobleman all kinds of welcoming gifts. The emperor gave him access to great riches and said to him: "Most worthy young man, fortune smiles upon you, and I greet you as my son, for as long as we both shall live. I propose to grant to you as fiefs so much of my land that you will be forever bound in happy alliance to me. All my affairs shall be yours, too. Most noble young man, God has sent you to be by my side. Govern well the peoples and the lands and help me maintain and preserve the stability of the realm so that no incursion or insurrection may ever harm it. For this, most worthy warrior, you will enjoy my faith and trust forever."

The emperor granted to Ernst and to his loyal followers all that they could wish for—it almost seemed too much to them. With all this, the duke was well aware that he was very much in the emperor's favor, and the emperor frequently showed him a fatherly concern. He treated the nobleman like his own son and was always concerned to enhance his standing and position. The emperor's relatives and vassals treated him the same way, and the emperor often summoned him to court to ask for his counsel. Whenever this happened, the emperor and the court invariably paid great attention to anything Ernst did or said.

His words of counsel were the wisest that anyone could give, and in every respect, Duke Ernst behaved impeccably.

He was, then, much favored by the emperor, something that the young warrior had earned through his good service to the state. The empress was equally pleased that her son was so much praised at court. Ernst's name stood at the head of the list of imperial counselors, some of whom had been his advisers for a very long time. The emperor showed him a great amount of favor and rewarded him well. The duke earned this in a number of difficult situations involving the emperor, and he regularly received gifts of large amounts of silver and gold. The noble duke, for his part, was completely loyal to the emperor without any conflict in all the time they were together. [558–645]

This state of affairs, however, had begun to irritate a certain Lord Henry, who would, prompted by the devil (who regularly causes conflicts and disruptions), bring about in a vicious manner the breakdown of the great bonds of friendship between them. This wretched evildoer was a relative of the emperor and also one of his counselors, and he spent his days thinking out ways of making the young nobleman look bad in the emperor's eyes, so that he would come to hate him. He did so purely and simply because Ernst enjoyed the emperor's favor to such a great extent. He therefore gave much thought to what he could say to make sure that he lost this favor and was damaged so much that the emperor turned against him. He and his associates were angry and bitter because he was no longer as well regarded at court as he had once been. This evil and untrustworthy man, the one I have just been describing, was the count palatine of the Rhine.

Ruthless and false, the wicked man went to the sovereign ruler of the empire and told him a lying tale of how Duke Ernst was only pretending to be loyal to the emperor. "You should know the truth," he said. "I have heard that he wants to remove you from the imperial throne. He wants to be as you are, to be as important and as rich. This disturbs me, my lord, and makes me uneasy. The problem is the many gifts of gold that you have given him. He has already bought the allegiance of all the princes, and you, my lord emperor, could lose your own position without someone who is more loyal at your side. He has been making loud noises about how he can match you in power, esteem, and noble birth, and all day and every day he talks about what he could do to take over your place and your throne. I was told all this, my lord, by someone who had actually heard him say all this, and he asked me to warn you secretly, before he made his move and supplanted you. If he were to drive you out, my lord, where should I be? I should be driven out as well. Most revered lord, think well before it is too late, so that we can stop this happening. If he were to become ruler of the empire, then he would take my position away from me, too, and the prospect fills me with terror."

The emperor was deeply shocked when he heard this tale and said: "I neither can nor will believe a story like the one you have just told me, that he should be as hostile to me as you have just claimed. It can only be jealousy and complete malice that has led to this accusation. You may take it from me that he could have done none of those things. He is a good and loyal man, solid and trustworthy, and he devotes all his efforts to assisting me and supporting the empire, and has done so willingly and in good faith up to now, so that I cannot possibly believe these wild tales about him. He is completely without malice, and there is no question of bad faith. His loyalty to me is something that I treasure, and I know that he is so steadfast that he would never have done those things. He is a fine warrior, and he has always stood by me and given me his support unstintingly. If you, sir, bear me as much love as he does, then stop spreading such tales. You are trying more and more to supplant him in my service. It would be extremely hard for me if I were to lose him, and you should drop this matter now."

"God save me, poor wretch that I am," said Count Henry of the Rhine, "and may heaven help us that Ernst has already been so effective in all his trickery that he has robbed you of your senses. I do know that I am your liegeman, bound in loyalty and friendship both to you and to the state, and I wish, as I may be saved, to stay that way. I am also a nobleman, from a noble family, with my own lands and properties, and I am acting in good faith in accordance with the law. If you could simply resist him, then I would have no need to worry, but if anything were to happen to you, your life, or your position, I should never get over it. If I had found Ernst here with you, then I would have confronted him on the spot with the treachery that he is harboring toward you, and he would not have been able to deny it. I have it from a completely reliable source, a man who swore on his own life that he had heard him say those things. You should know that it strikes at my very heart that you do not believe me. You must understand that you are putting your own life and position in danger. My lord and emperor, you must proceed with great caution and guard yourself and your position with well-advised circumspection. If they were all to move against you together with armed forces, it will be too late, and we shall have no defense against them. Meanwhile, he has such a powerful army because he has won all the princes over to his side, so that they can ride in arms against you and set the whole state in flames."

When the emperor heard this, the whole pack of lies affected him so much that he conceived in his heart a great anger against the duke, and he came to believe that all the things the count, his kinsman, had told him were true, and he became dejected and depressed. "May God reward you, most noble knight," he said, "for showing such concern for me. If I am spared, he shall suffer for this. He will never raise himself up so high that I cannot drive him down and bring about his fall, and my empire shall have peace again."

The emperor was now patently very angry, but the treacherous vassal said: "Do not show so much anger, but follow the advice I am going to give you. You can punish him easily and without harm to yourself. You must keep all that I have told you secret from the empress and from your court, or else someone might warn him. Then you need to make sure that he is brought down before he notices that anything is wrong. You need to take the castles in his own duchy, and strike before he can raise his own forces and defend himself. We have to invade his lands with an army because if he were able to mount a counterattack, it would cause enormous damage to the empire itself. His people are solidly behind him and will flock to him in large numbers, but you can take action without serious damage to yourself. You should gather together your forces, but do it in secret, so that no one has any idea of who it is that you are planning to fight or where your campaign is headed until you have actually done him some damage. He will not be able to do anything about it because his defenses will not be ready. This, lord, is my advice: try and take his castles with promises of friendship, so that they do not help him in any conflict. Then our bold warrior will not be able to fight back and will have to flee the country to escape." [646–852]

The emperor at once agreed to Count Henry's plan and did what he had advised, although later on he would regret doing so, because he suffered for it. He assembled a large army, however, and sent it into action against the duke, moving against his stepson with fire and the sword. All that the duke could do against this was to fortify and defend his own palace. Attack and devastation soon made him forget any love he may have had for the emperor. The count palatine caused a great deal of damage to towns and castles in the duke's lands and indeed occupied some of them with his own forces, while he had others burned down. And all this was done on the basis of a pack of lies!

When Count Henry had brought great devastation and fire to many parts of the lands, he laid siege to the city of Nuremberg, attacking it fiercely. He discovered, however, that the city was home to a large number of bold warriors, ready to defend it with their lives. They managed to bring down many of those attacking from all sides, sappers and those with scaling ladders, but the greatest number of those killed were those trying to storm the city gates. Count Henry himself led the attack, carrying the imperial banner, and he knew well how to urge his men on. Raw recruits and experienced soldiers joined in the melee, and there were very many losses before they were able to retreat, get away from the fortified city, and go back to break their own camp. They escaped, but only with considerable difficulty, and Nuremberg was not taken.

The count continued for any number of days and weeks with his marauding sallies into the duke's territories and did not meet with resistance. The devastation of the lands was huge—villages, mansions, and towns were destroyed, and nothing could stop him. The noble, bold, and brave Duke Ernst of Bavaria knew that he was up against the might of the empire and took counsel with the best men that he still had with him as to what they should now do. Earl Wetzel, his loyal vassal, said: "If you put up a resistance now it will be very difficult for you to justify yourself in legal terms because it would look as if you are guilty of making an attack on the state itself. You need to try to get back in favor in the eyes of the state. But if, after all, the emperor wants to destroy you," the noble warrior went on, "it's clear then he can do so by force. I would advise you not to fight against him anymore, because even if you had a thousand times more troops it would still not be worth opposing him. He could perhaps stop his attacks if he would agree to a parley, so stand your troops down for the moment. If he nevertheless wants to drive you out, then you need to defend yourself as strongly as possible. Before he drives you out of the empire and your own lands, he should learn that you can cause him a lot of damage. We are not going to be driven into exile quite so easily, and we can still defend ourselves. Meanwhile, however, you should try to find out from our own lady, the empress, what is behind all this and why you are being treated this way. That," said the noble warrior, "is my advice." [853–948]

The duke then sent a messenger to his mother and asked her to tell him what lay behind all this, and to complain about all the damage that was being inflicted upon him so unjustly. The message was taken by a good and entirely trustworthy knight, who set off at once, and with great care and cunning managed to get to the empress and make his report. She listened to him with tears in her eyes and told the messenger to stay that night, concealed in her quarters. Then she went to talk to the emperor when she knew she would find him alone and said, choosing her words carefully: "Most noble sovereign, I implore you on your own honor and in the name of Almighty God to grant me leave to speak. My son Ernst sends words of complaint about the harm you have done to him, and that he has lost your favor through no fault of his own. He cannot understand why he should have forfeited your goodwill, and why you should now want in your anger to dispossess him of his own duchy and destroy him, without any regard for the due process of law. The noble duke requests, therefore, that you permit him to come before you. If anyone can produce evidence of his having gone against you, then he will make amends, as is the law for all men. Whatever you demand of him he will carry out if you will show him your mercy and grant him sufficient time to prove to you in peace that he is completely loyal to you, and that he has always been completely loyal, without any trace of deceit."

But the mighty emperor answered her grimly and angrily, and with great discourtesy: "You must not ask that of me, because I cannot accede to your request. Madam, your son has committed such a great offense against me that he can—and he may be certain of this—never be admitted to my presence again. While there is breath in my body I shall make sure that he is fully aware of the harm he has done me—make no mistake about that! I shall despoil his lands, and he will find me an implacable enemy for the whole of my life. I mean what I say."

When the noble lady became aware of just how grim the mood of the emperor was, she was very shaken and did not dare to continue pleading for her son. With womanly dignity she withdrew at once to her own chambers and sent the messenger swiftly back to Bavaria to tell her son that Count Henry had poisoned the mind of the emperor so much against him that in all honesty no one could now help him. "It is up to you now to act like a true hero and protect your lands and your own reputation as much as you are able. The emperor is furious and has declared publicly that if you do not leave the country, he will have your life and strip you of all your titles and honors." The empress told the messenger that that was what he should say.

When he heard this, the messenger set off home as quickly as he could and was soon back in Bavaria, where he found his lord in one of his castles. Ernst asked him if he had found out why the emperor was now his implacable enemy, and his brave vassal told him: "I can give you a full report. First, the empress, your mother, assures you of her love, and asks that you should assert and justify yourself. A great deal of damage has been done to you through no fault of your own, and Henry, the count palatine, has covertly ensured that you have lost entirely the emperor's support. Most bold warrior, you should now consider how to defeat him. The wretch wants to deprive you of your inheritance, and if you do nothing it will forever be a matter of regret for you. Your lady mother told me further that she had heard for certain that no one can help you, and that the emperor is determined to be your sworn enemy. Brave warrior that you are, you must show that you have always been a noble warrior. The emperor is doing you wrong, and God will help you all the more willingly because of that. With God's help, then, even if the emperor does drive you out, you can make sure that men always say that you were true to the lands that you inherited and that the emperor forced you to leave. But this is not—the lady said—her only advice. You should also try something else. Make it known to the princes of the empire, whom the emperor has summoned to himself, I think for an advisory meeting with him, that they should be kind enough to plead your case. Let him hear how they speak of you—he should judge you on that evidence." That, then, was the message brought back to the noble duke. [949–1092]

Ernst now sent off another messenger, who left immediately to go and meet with the great nobles, which happened at night. Once the messenger had spoken to them and reported on the perilous situation, as his lord had instructed him, they were much concerned about the dangerous position into which Ernst had been placed through no fault of his own, and promised that they would willingly speak out on his behalf. Early the following morning, straight after Mass, they came to court and went to the emperor. They threw themselves at his feet and made their request: "Lord, since we have to make an entreaty to you, please hear us out, as custom demands, without letting us feel your anger." The emperor replied, "Stand up, and if you have a request, then you may make it." One of the princes then said: "We beg of you, most noble emperor, that in the name of Almighty God you should look with favor again on Duke Ernst, against whom you have been turned by lies and calumnies, and who has lost your grace through no fault of his own. But lost it he has, and he has no idea why, and therefore, we, your princes, wish to plead in this place that you may consider granting him the grace that he seeks from you. We are prepared to help him make amends for any wrongs he has done you until we are able to change your mind and calm your anger, and in accord with your will, your judgment, and your choice, take the pain from your heart for the honor of the empire itself. Let him, lord, appear before you. Let him do whatever penance you think fit for any wrongs he has done you, and we shall be in your debt forevermore. Do not let him, noble lord, perish as an innocent man. In all loyalty he entreats you for grace, and will devote all his lands and goods to the effort of regaining your favor. Grant him a period of truce so that we can bring him to you for a formal hearing. For any other demands that you may have of him, we shall stand as guarantors."

The emperor replied immediately in an uncourtly outburst of anger: "You go too far in what you ask. I have sworn oaths in this case that can never be rescinded. He will get no truce and no reconciliation, and anyone with any love for me and for the state cannot make such a request and still remain my friend. Ernst wants to depose me and set himself up as my equal in power and control. On my life, he shall suffer for that! One of us must drive the other out, and that is what he has to know. Any prince who encourages him in his conflict with me will always be my enemy, you may be sure of that!"

The princes stood up. They had to abandon their petition for fear of the emperor; however friendly they might have been with the duke before, and however much they may have wanted to give him support, they had to join the campaign against him. They did not dare to put up any more defenses, and they all had to abandon him, and on the emperor's command even his relatives were forced to bear arms against him.

This would lead to great suffering all over Germany, because Duke Ernst defended himself bravely against the forces of the state for six whole years, until he was ultimately defeated and forced into exile because he could no longer resist the strength of his enemies and the power of the state. [1093–1196]

CHAPTER 2

THE REBEL

Now, however, when the messenger returned, and Duke Ernst had heard the verdict, the popular leader declared: "Now we are in God's hands, and we ask Him to grant us that we take our revenge on the faithless wretch whose fault it is that I have to endure all this pain and suffering. I have never posed any threat of damage to the state. I promise you that the count will pay for lies and slander that he has used to alienate me from my dearly loved emperor, whom I have always honored with complete loyalty, and his sorrows were always my sorrows, too." The confident warrior went on: "I am forced now to think of attack. I shall be happy if I can redeem myself with honor. God knows the truth, that I did not throw away the favor of the emperor by some foolish action. He has now given free rein to his anger with me, but he should hear and be well aware, whether he likes it or not, that I propose to remain for the time being here in his empire with him, unless prevented by some complete disaster, sickness, poverty, or death—things like that can always happen. I have plenty of valiant fighters who will not let me be driven out while there is breath in their bodies, so that I can put up a resistance. There is also no question," continued the brave warrior, "that he might take away the lands that have come down to me by right of birth. He has no feudal justification in that respect."

The emperor was holding court at Speyer in the palatinate. When the duke was told of this, he thought: "I have to go there regardless of any danger to myself. I must cross the Rhine and get to my enemies, the ones who have done me so much harm." And so he selected two of his vassals, men in whose bravery he was completely confident, and rode off with them. When they had crossed the Rhine, he explained to his two companions what he had in mind and wanted to do. They approved of his plan. It was very late when they reached the court, and Ernst took Earl Wetzel with him while the second warrior companion was detailed to look after the horses and to keep a careful watch so that he would be armed and ready if needed, and they could get away before being captured. The angry duke hurried to the rooms of the emperor, the head of the state. There were chamberlains at the door, but they were not guarding it well. The duke and the earl found the door unbarred. Things went better for them than they could ever have wished. Emperor Otto sat in this room alone in discussion with Count Henry, his kinsman. The two valiant knights rushed into the room with drawn swords and brought the discussion to a harsh end. The sovereign just managed to escape, jumping up from his seat and across a bench. It seemed to him to take an inordinate amount of time, but he managed to get to a chapel. Count Henry, the emperor's vassal, now paid for the advice he had given as the duke struck him such a fierce blow that he fell to the ground, his head severed from his body.

"It was a bad day for the emperor when he accepted what you had to say," declared the duke. "He's the one I was after, but he got away, or he would have met a grim death from my hand. He deserves the dangerous position he is now in because he always believed you. God damn you, why did you treat me that way, you devil! I never caused any harm to you or to anyone else, and for that I should have enjoyed your praise, and that of the state. Now you are lying there blood-soaked and pitiful—that's what you have achieved. You had no cause to turn against me, and a lot of men have died because of your lying words. Now may Almighty God have mercy on your soul."

No one appeared, and the warrior made his way back to the horses. The three men mounted and rode off as fast as they could so that the bold fighters would not have to engage in battle. It was a very dark night, which helped them get back safely across the Rhine. After this, the duke defended his lands bravely and well until he was forced into exile.

There was a great outcry in all the castles of the palatinate when it became known that the bold Duke Ernst had killed Count Henry, and there was much weeping and wailing. They were amazed that he had managed to escape. In the general hue and cry all roads far and wide were searched by well-armed soldiers with spears and shields, but they were unable to trace them or catch them up. When they found nothing, they returned to the city in despair at not being able to pursue them, but no matter how much they might have bemoaned the fact, the three men had made it to safety. [1197–1350]

Now that Duke Ernst had taken his revenge, and the emperor realized that his kinsman was dead, but that the duke had escaped clean away, the emperor gave vent to his sorrow. "For your sake, my most worthy warrior, we shall hunt him down without ceasing. He has filled my whole heart with sadness and regret, and I mourn your death! I shall never be truly happy again until I have avenged your death so fully that it will be talked about forever. If I am spared, and even if all my people, all my vassals and all my friends should desert me, I shall make my way as quickly as I can into his homeland. Let my cries of pain and shame rise up to God in heaven. I call upon all those who are my friends to punish him for coming to my court to commit such a dreadful deed. It will be a great sorrow to me for my whole life that he dared perpetrate this outrage on one of my relatives. He shall learn for certain that he can never be forgiven for this. Not in living memory has the ruler of a land been treated in this manner. I shall never be rid of the shame that I had to suffer such an outrage in the presence of my entire court."

This was the emperor's misery. He gave orders that the body should be laid out with dignity, and set the customary ceremonial watch over the body during the night. The next morning, Henry was buried with great ceremony. After that, Otto called all the nobles to him at court and told them all, both the high-ranking and those of minor degree, of the great loss inflicted upon him at his own court so maliciously by Duke Ernst and Earl Wetzel, his vassal, and how they had done him such shameful harm that he would never be able to forget this as long as he lived. Never would he be able to forgive Ernst for the crime of murdering his kinsman, but there was also a worse crime, that they had come close to killing him, and had he not taken refuge in the chapel, he would have lost his life. "My warriors," he said, "you should react with fury that he has so shamefully and wickedly committed such an outrage against all of you and against the state." It was decided at once that he should be condemned, and that his lands, fiefs, and property, and all that he had inherited, should be forfeit. "You have every right, lord," declared many of the nobles, "that he should be brought down by any means possible. It is the punishment that he deserves." The emperor formally declared Duke Ernst and his companions outlaws to the state, and before he left the court assembly on the Rhine, he called for a military campaign by the princes and nobles against the duke's lands. Every one of them was summoned to join this, young and old, as long as they were ready and able to bear arms. He gathered together a great many fierce warriors in the territories of the German empire, more than thirty thousand first-class fighters. The most high-ranking of the princes brought plenty of good warriors, all equipped and ready for battle. The emperor then gave the order for the army to set out under his banner to attack their enemy, the duke, in his own land of Bavaria. They reached Regensburg, which was placed under siege by a powerful force of men. Many bold warriors suffered death when they fell in the battles there.

The imperial standard was carried by powerful supporters, as is always the case with this kind of attack. A great many fierce warriors donned their shining chain mail, and these proud young men encircled the city walls and launched an attack on them, storming from all sides. A lot of men, noble and otherwise, lost their lives in the attack. The duke's men raised a green banner and assembled in full force at the city gates, where they came face to face with their sovereign and his men. They caused a great deal of damage when they engaged with the attackers—they clashed violently in the storm of battle, with sharp swords striking against shining helmets as one army struggled against the other. Many warriors were cut down and bloodied, and there were many blows returned with interest. Fighters tested their very lives in the cause of glory in battle, and deep wounds were cut through the chain mail they wore, although the young and bold warriors paid them no heed. They cut and thrust with swords and spears, and many of the attackers and the defenders were wounded. A great number of those carried off the field of battle slept the long, cold sleep of death.

The battle raged on until nightfall, and both sides fought vigorously, with no difference between the imperial troops and the defenders, until the darkness enveloped them all. The defenders retreated into the city, and the attackers had to set up a large number of tents and huts all around it on the battlefield. Those who lay dead, killed in valiant struggle, were carried away on stretchers. The defenders of the city had inflicted such pain on the besiegers that the emperor had cause for great regret—he lost more than a thousand men in the attack. This depressed him and caused him great anguish, but also anger. Later there would be still more losses of those who died of the wounds suffered in the battle.

The records tell that the defenders of the city also suffered losses, with many dead and wounded, something they had to struggle to come to terms with, but they were forced to accept it because that is what so often happens in war. The emperor and his forces now laid heavy siege to the city, and the citizens set up their defenses on the towers and the battlements and made it very clear to him that they were going to offer resistance. As a result, the entire imperial force prepared for a mass assault, knights and common soldiery alike, and moved in on all sides close to the walls. This caused a great many casualties among the attackers. Arrows and spears rained down from the towers, and rocks were hurled from the openings in the battlements. Many a man hurtled, fatally wounded, into the defensive ditch as a result of being part of the attack. Shining chain mail became red with blood, and proud young warriors who had looked for glory in battle found death instead. [1351–1554]

The emperor became increasingly angry when he had to keep his armies outside Regensburg for more than six months. He was, however, extremely distressed by the extent of their losses and wanted to take his revenge for it all on this great city. He quickly had rams, movable coverings, and mobile siege engines built and made ready for the long battle. When he was unable to subdue the city, and the citizens refused to surrender, he got his brave soldiers to bring these siege engines right up to the ditch, and a particularly fierce attack was launched against the city. The valiant townspeople manned the battlements. However large the army may have been that had been brought in from outside their country, they defended their walls with great bravery. But the battle cost them dearly, and they fell like snow. You could hear the screams of those who could no longer withstand the attack. Then the emperor sent in his entire force on the attack. They shattered the parapets with stones hurled by their mangonels so much that there was little left of them, then smashed them with more shots from their siege engines. The citizens would have liked to sue for peace because they were so frightened of all this weaponry that the enemy was using against them, and they lost a great number of their fighters. The attack went on all day, from early morning till nightfall with undiminished ferocity, and did not stop until it was completely dark.

Those in the city made use of the cover of night to send out a messenger in secret to find Duke Ernst to give a report and to ask him how they could save themselves. They were no longer able to defend the city and would otherwise have to die there. With enormous effort they had withstood the attack so far but could no longer hold out. At this, the noble duke agreed that he would rather surrender the city than lose any more of those in it. "Never mind where I am, let them now treat with the enemy so that they can leave the city with their lives, and calm the emperor's fury, because his great anger is directed at me."

The messenger returned quickly and made his report, and at dawn on the following day the emperor received word that the citizens wished to place themselves at his mercy if he would let the defending soldiers live and permit them to return to their homes unharmed. The besieging army approved thoroughly of this because their own losses had been so great. The emperor asked the senior nobles for their opinion on what was the best course, and they all agreed that they would welcome this. "So be it, then" declared the emperor.

As was mentioned before, when the peace treaty was concluded and the emperor had given his hand upon it, he had his standard raised on one of the high towers and rode into the city. Some were unhappy about this state of affairs, but it simply had to be, since he himself had besieged the city. They had defended themselves against the imperial force for so many days, but had been unable to fight against the state any longer. They had fought so valiantly against the opposing forces that it was apparent how good they were as warriors. It was a matter of great delight to the emperor and his followers that they had taken the city. The warriors' lives were spared, and those wishing to leave were allowed to go wherever they liked. Those who had joined the emperor in the campaign were now also relieved. Some of these had, however, received wounds from which they would not recover. The mighty emperor installed his men in the city and left. The camp of the besieging army was struck, the temporary lodgings burned, and they moved away. Now the sun shone on bright ring mail, and the imperial standard fluttered above the large and powerful army, and many warriors followed that standard.

The ruler of the empire now moved in an angry mood through the duke's lands. They were burned and pillaged, and a great deal of damage was caused as castles and towns were sacked. Ernst had to suffer all this because the power of the emperor was so great that he could not withstand the attacks. Otto did not want to leave anything of the duke's but wanted him to lose everything, and he gave vent to his fury by laying waste to the land, although he had to pay for it with the loss of many of his own fighters, who did not manage to come home alive. He had no intention of forgiving the duke for any of the harm he had caused him. The duke's troops battled on bravely because they did not want their land to be destroyed. They put up a bold resistance for as long as they could and as long as they were able to fight.

When it became clear to Duke Ernst that his lands had been ravaged and his castles taken, the brave lord was sorry for his men, who had stood with him throughout his misfortunes, ready to fight to the death. He had always looked after them, and they in their turn had supported him day and night in his attempt to avenge the wrong done to him. So now he rode into the imperial lands, and his people attacked and pillaged just as much, and so it went on, back and forth. He sacked a good number of castles, and whenever he got the upper hand, he brought down the emperor's supporters and killed some of them. He did the emperor plenty of damage. Those who had taken up arms against him were made to lose their lands and property. In this way the bold warrior-duke waged for five years and more his war against the empire and its forces, asserting himself vigorously against them, such that none of them could, by any means at all, drive him out. He was able, by force of arms and by strategy, to maintain his position. His followers continued to support him, fighting for his reputation down to the point where the duke had used up all his resources in the pursuit of the war, until he at last had to give way and withdraw. [1555–1738]

When the noble Ernst was no longer able to pursue his war against the state, he took a wise decision, now that he was forced to give up. He called all his warriors together, the very best ones, whose fighting spirit he knew well, and from these battle-hardened fighters he chose fifty of the very finest, men who had never let him down and who had never given way in any fight. His idea was that they should leave the country together with him. "You are my closest friends," he said, "and have never let me down in any desperate situation, and have always stood bravely by my side. I want to ask for your advice, because you have always behaved loyally toward me. My lands are in ruins, wrecked and pillaged, and I have exhausted all my resources. My adherents want gold from me, because they are assuming that I still have great quantities of it. But because of the war," he went on, "I have nothing left. The emperor and all his adherents are my enemies, and I know full well that they are united in their opposition to me. Sadly, I can no longer offer any resistance to the imperial forces. I have accomplished a lot by resisting for so long, and whenever people hear of it they marvel, and it is greatly due to the fact that you have supported me so nobly. But now I must out of fear and necessity yield to the emperor. If you swim against the current you can manage it for a time, but I can tell you that eventually you will be forced downstream. I am afraid that that's my situation now, that we have reached that point. If you fight against the state, you may be able to last out for a time, but in the end you will have to give way, and that seems to be where I am now."

"We fought so fiercely against the forces of the empire and did so much damage to the emperor's men that I can no longer stay here. We have exhausted ourselves with war and used up all our resources, and it could well be the end of us. If we could get hold of supplies, as we did when we were able to defeat the enemy, and replenish our coffers, then we might still survive and defend ourselves against the enemy. But now it makes sense for us to escape from the emperor. We can no longer offer resistance, and my firm intent is to go overseas. If you, my lords, think this is the right thing to do, then we shall act in God's name and undertake a crusade, go and serve the Holy Sepulchre. In that way we can withdraw with honor before they have a chance to drive us out. In any case, we have offended against God, and should do penance for that, so that He might forgive us, and we may regain His grace. If we survive and one day return to this country, then perhaps everything will be returned to us that the emperor has taken. Now I ask you all, vassals and kinsmen alike, that you do not let me go alone out of this land. You, my warriors, would be doing good works and earning esteem, and for your loyalty I shall reward you, service for service."

Thus spoke the noble knight. His brave warriors all agreed, saying that the idea was divinely inspired and that they would risk their lives for their lord duke, entrusting to God's care their wives and children at home and staying with him as they traveled in God's name across the sea. Nothing but death, they all promised, would prevent them from going with him on his journey.

Now there was no further delay, and the duke and his companions set off happily and formally took the Cross. The news—and it was welcomed by everyone—soon came to his lands that their warrior-duke had taken the Cross, and that fifty of his knights had gone with him, chosen by their lord to go on this journey to serve God across the seas. At this, a good many more declared themselves ready to go. Duke Ernst took great care with the equipment—shining hauberks, firm steel helmets, and sharp swords, everything as appropriate for these splendid fighting men. Thus well equipped, they left the imperial lands, and it may truly be said that in no time and place was a party ever better equipped to venture abroad. No one, unless they were entirely malicious, could have dared say that these warriors were leaving their lands because of their poverty. That was clear.

And so they prepared for their journey abroad, many of the knights rejoicing in the fact that they could serve God by going with the party. Plenty of bold warriors from the whole of the German empire were happy to join Duke Ernst's expedition. His mother, the empress, sent him five hundred gold pieces and much valuable material—ermines and silk clothes decorated with gold thread, and also valuable bedding. Ernst accepted these gifts with grateful thanks and shared everything with his companions. In every respect he was an ideal nobleman, and he could do nothing about the fact that he was being driven out unjustly. While he had remained in the country he had faced so much adversity that his deeds will be talked about forever.

CHAPTER 3

THE
EXILE

The day approached on which the duke and his men intended to set out to go across the sea. A great number of warriors from different places who knew him rallied to him with their followers and begged him in the name of God and his own nobility that he should grant them the favor of letting them come with him, because they knew that he would protect them against any dangers that might face them. They wanted him to accept them into his service and to go with him to Jerusalem, to support him in anything he undertook and never abandon him whatever the dangers. They wished to be his men, devoting their lives and their property to him in any perilous situation, even in the face of death. "That," they said, "is our one desire above all else." "I understand," replied the valiant duke, "and I welcome you, my dear friends, in God's name. You may be assured that I shall never let you down as long as I live. You will be rewarded, and all things shall be shared with you—anything large or small that God grants me shall be yours as well as mine. For as long as I live you shall not regret making cause with, and placing your trust in, me. I will gladly take you on as companions and brothers, showing special favors to none—you shall all be equals on this journey, and you may be assured that I shall do my utmost to protect you day and night." The knights thanked him, and the duke was delighted that he now had acquired so many fine men for his retinue. His company now contained a good thousand experienced warriors who would now travel abroad with him, and they had all sworn oaths of loyal allegiance to him as their captain and leader.

Duke Ernst was ready to set out on the journey in princely fashion, and once he had taken formal leave and departed, all his relatives and feudal dependents were extremely sad to see him go—all those who held him dear were desperately unhappy, since their noble lord had always cared for and protected them faithfully while he ruled over them. When the great lord and warrior, bold and unafraid, left the country, he handed over control of his castles and territories, his properties and his feudal dependents to relatives, wanting them to have care of them so that they would not be taken away from him at some point.

And the great Duke Ernst, with his noble warrior companions, took leave of his homeland. [1739–1998]

Ernst was pleased that his retinue was so large and that a powerful army followed him on the long journey to the sea. They set off in good spirits. Earl Wetzel, his feudal retainer, was an exceptional warrior, and the duke put him in command of the army of followers. He carried out this duty in exemplary fashion, and they were such a strong military force that they were never attacked. They reached Hungary in good spirits. When news came to the king of Hungary, the arrival of the duke was welcomed heartily, because the king had heard of Ernst's boldness and of how he had resolutely defended himself for so long in the face of imperial opposition. He received the duke and his whole entourage well, and when they arrived, he invited them into his presence and treated them with great honor, for which they thanked him greatly. The king provided quarters for them and was happy to give the duke gifts and an honorable passage through his lands. Ernst accepted the gifts and took his leave of the king in good spirits. The king assisted their journey through the forests of Bulgaria, and thus the brave warriors were happy to reach the empire of the Byzantine Greeks.

And so the army arrived safely at the city of Constantinople. Ernst instructed his field marshal Wetzel and his men to go on ahead without delay and look for quarters, so that when they all arrived, they would have somewhere to rest. Their arrival, however, was soon reported to the ruler of the Eastern Empire, who took great pains to accommodate the duke and his men, because he, too, had heard of him and knew that he had been driven unjustly into exile and that he had fought against the emperor Otto and the Western Empire itself but had departed with honor from that country. Therefore, he instructed his people to look after Duke Ernst and his men well for as long as they stayed, and this was carried out assiduously. All the people, rich or poor, treated them even better than instructed, and they did everything for them.

The noble duke stayed there for a little over three weeks before he was able to procure a ship that would be suitable to carry the men, plus provisions, and their equipment, and eventually he found a ship that seemed suitable for the voyage. The noble Byzantine ruler had them conducted to the ship and provided a six-month supply of fresh food for them. He also gave them gold from his own coffers. He endeared himself greatly to the duke by these great acts of kindness. When everything was ready for them to set sail, the noble Duke Ernst went to the mighty ruler of Byzantium and asked formal permission to take his leave, now that they were well prepared and provisioned for their journey. "This has been made possible by your great generosity," said the noble warrior, "and for the rest of our lives we shall forever be grateful to you for it and be in your debt, praying always to God to keep you. And now let us bid you farewell."

The Byzantine ruler gave them yet more of his gold, which was taken to Ernst's ship, and then he said: "May God permit every one of you to travel safely in His service and keep and protect you as you serve Him, so that we may rejoice with you. That is our wish for you and your men." With that, Duke Ernst left his imperial host, and he and his men went on board in good spirits. The Greeks had taken the duke and his men to their hearts, and to demonstrate their love and friendship a vast number of Greeks set out with them in more than fifty ships, placing themselves under his command. They vowed that with their help the great warrior would come safely to the Holy Land.

Once all the farewells had been said and everyone had embarked, the sails were hoisted, and the noble knights set off toward Syria. They were well provisioned and sailed on contentedly and without any worries. When they had been on the high seas for five days, however, the pilgrim travelers had cause for tears of anguish, because a violent storm blew up and drove the ships apart so that they could no longer be seen by each other. Twelve of them were sunk straightaway, and all on them were drowned, suffering a dreadful death. The rest had to face terrible dangers on the raging seas. All those following the duke were driven so far apart that none of them saw any of the others ever again. This was an enormous tragedy for Duke Ernst. He was devastated that because of this he had been separated from all the Greek warriors when the storm winds drove them all away across the wild waves.

The brave hero had, however, cleverly managed in all this to gather with him onto a single ship the bold warriors who had accompanied him from Germany or who had joined him since then, and later he would have cause to be pleased that they had stayed together in this way. But now they were driven on the wild seas to places where no men had sailed before or since, and where the great hero and his men had to suffer enormous misfortunes, coming face to face with grim death. It can truly be said of all they suffered that no one has ever heard of greater tribulations than those that would be faced by Duke Ernst.

The duke and his men sailed for over three months on the open sea without the noble warriors ever making landfall, and this caused Ernst great anxiety, because their supply of provisions was by now nearly exhausted, and they had begun to think that they would never survive. Every one of the men was worried, but then, early one morning, just around dawn, the skies began to clear, and their problems were over. The morning sun rose in the sky, and the weather was really fine, as is often the case after a storm. The sea was clear and calm, and even the wind, which had tossed them about so violently, had now dropped. The warriors now became aware that things were getting much better as they suddenly got sight of a beautiful country, which pleased them enormously. This country was called Grippia. [1999–2206]

CHAPTER 4

THE CITADEL OF THE CRANES

They made a course for this country, steering the ship toward land, and sailed into a harbor where they dropped anchor. Once on terra firma, they very soon saw an extremely fine city surrounded by an impressive wall, finely decorated with the most beautiful shining yellow and green marble, with black, red, and white insets making up striking checkered patterns, as well as a great many images of things both strange and familiar, some known to them only by hearsay, and all as clear as glass. The whole was surrounded by a deep defensive ditch full of water so that the whole city was surrounded by a moat. The battlements were also built and decorated magnificently, gilded, and decorated with all kinds of artistically arranged precious stones. This magnificent citadel had nothing to fear from any attackers. The towers, defensive parapets, and firing-ports were carefully planned and arranged—so we are told in the books in which the city is described. We must be grateful to the person who passed this story on to us for giving us such a clear picture. Amazing people, too, lived in the shining city.

When our brave warriors reached land, then, they took in the sails, dropped anchor at once, and put out the boat. Duke Ernst said to his friends and companions: "It seems that things have turned out well, now that God has sent us to this beautiful country and fine-looking city. We had very few provisions left, and we can replenish our supplies here so that we do not starve. We have had to suffer a lot since we took to the seas and had no sight of any land, but now that we have found this amazing-looking city, I am confident that there will be people in charge there, and we shall find out today whether they are Christians or pagans. We shall have to approach them diplomatically so that they will sell us the provisions we need. If they are not Christians they will not let us live, but it is just as well if we lose our lives here—we set out to fight for God, and we should not complain if we fall in battle rather than starving to death on the ship."

When the men heard this, they agreed: "Yes, we came with no other aim than to fight for God, and we will gladly suffer death in His service, and always accept joy and pain alike willingly for His sake." The brave and resolute warriors armed themselves well, put on their shining hauberks, took their weapons, and got into the boats. When they reached the shore, Duke Ernst unfolded his standard, which was scarlet, and gave it to Earl Wetzel as its bearer. Then the warrior led them boldly forward, all fully armed with helmets and shields, across the open land. He carried the standard proudly up to the gates of the city, where the men now assembled.

The gates of the city stood wide open. The bold warriors had, however, seen no one on the city walls, neither inside nor outside, and they found this very puzzling. They said to themselves: "What does this mean? They must be strange people if they do not let themselves be seen. Perhaps they have hidden themselves to gain some time. They want to trick us into entering the city so that they can overcome us more easily if we are inside the walls. There is no other reason why they should not show themselves. But they should be careful, because we could still do them a lot of harm—we could kill and hack to pieces a good number of them before they manage to kill us."

Duke Ernst now said: "Let us make a start by trying to get hold of some wine, some bread, and other provisions before they try to kill us. We are well armed in good ring mail and ready for battle, so the young warriors should form up and carry the standard across the bridge into the city gates. Before they realize what is going on and try to drive us away, we can, my brave fighters, get in by force of arms. And so you bold warriors should now force your way into this citadel in such a way that they will always remember us as dangerous and difficult guests."

The fierce and resolute warriors rallied around the standard, which the bold earl carried so fearlessly, and he led the band of exiles through the gates and into the city.

There was no one there.

They hurried onward, rushing into the city itself, but there was no one to offer resistance in any way. And so, without a single battle, the warriors reached the center of the city, still expecting someone to come to meet them. In a green circular garden, cool and shaded from the sun, they found tables and chairs set out, and no emperor, however rich and powerful, ever enjoyed such a splendid setting. Our young warriors saw a ring of beautifully decorated tables covered with cloths edged with the finest gold braid. The seats were all splendid, too, and I can tell you that the tables were impressively laid out. On every one of them they saw meat—both game and farmed—bread, fish, and a huge variety of the very best drinks, meads and wines made from different fruits. Where they acquired all this in that country is a mystery. The goblets and plates were of gold, the dishes of finely chased silver. They found here everything you could possibly want, and Duke Ernst said to his men: "You would be wise to take all the food you need and give thanks to Our Lord for the rich gifts that He has bestowed on us today. If we find something," he went on, "that will serve as food for us, then we may take it without sinning, but you must leave everything else. God may be testing us, so you should leave the gold and silver and the valuable cloths entirely alone. We should give thanks to Our Lord, who has saved us so often and who has bestowed this food upon us. We were in desperate need, defenseless against death by starvation out on the wild ocean. We should all give special thanks for the great miracle that God has shown us. Now go to the tables and eat happily and restore yourselves, and when you have done that, my advice is to load the ship with enough food for the time it will take before God brings us to Jerusalem. We cannot," said the duke, "stay here beyond daybreak. Be aware that we should then set off again, because I am sure that this city is not completely empty. Its inhabitants are not very far away. We have to take into account," said their young leader, "that they could be upon us at any moment."

The bold warriors washed their hands, then they sat down at the tables and ate and drank until they were no longer hungry. However much they consumed, there was still plenty for all. Then when they had finished eating, the bold warriors got up from the tables, and all of them, the younger men and those who were more experienced, wandered around the city and inspected all the marvelous decorations in gold and precious stones. And when they had done that, they came to a house in which—thanks be to God—they found meat, wine, and bread, though it would be impossible to describe accurately just how much was stored there. A king and his entire army would have found sufficient supplies there. This delighted them, and they began to load provisions onto their ship, something they did very quickly. After that, they went back to rest, and left the beautiful city open and empty. In good spirits the warriors went back to their ship and took their ease after all their efforts.

When they had rested for a time and felt better, Duke Ernst suddenly said to Earl Wetzel, his chief of staff: "I should much like to go back once more and have a closer look at the city, however dangerous it might be, since it is such a splendid place. If you want to come with me, tell me now." "I do indeed," replied the Earl. "Of course I will come with you, even if it were to cost me my life. You should, my lord, also ask all of our close companions in this brotherhood for the sake of their own honor and in the name of God to make themselves ready to rally to the flag at once if they realize we are in trouble, and to come and help save us immediately they hear the noise of any fighting. The city is large and looks powerful, and we should take a close look at it. I cannot imagine that there are no people there. Whatever their reasons might be for not showing themselves, I would guess that they want to observe and see what we are going to do. If they are not going to attack us, well, we must find out what they have in mind for us. May God protect us! Whatever they may intend, however, we must, for better or worse, go back there. We must make the attempt, even if we don't come out of it alive." The warriors at once agreed that they would help in any emergency or would die in the attempt.

When they went back to the city, they discovered a great many beautiful features, gold decorations, and they gazed at all kinds of works of art made of gold and precious stones. They noticed a large number of sumptuous palaces, all wonderfully well constructed. Furthermore, the warriors found arches and high gateways that glittered like the stars, finer than any that could be seen anywhere on earth. The buildings were as beautifully decorated inside as outside, and everywhere they found vast and stately rooms. This most marvelously built city lay so near to the sea that even if a great king with his entire army tried to attack it, he would be driven away.

When they had seen all these wonders, they hurried on to the circular gardens where they had eaten earlier. When they walked around them, they saw that quite near to these gardens was a splendid palace, positively covered in gold, with the walls studded all over with glistening green emeralds. Then the bold and worthy Duke Ernst found a beautifully proportioned room, furnished very richly and again decorated with precious stones, beautifully and expertly set in bright gold. They went into the room and saw there (according to our source) a magnificently upholstered bed, decorated once more with gold panels, richly and tastefully set with pearls and other jewels. The shining gold chasings on the bedposts were engraved with images of lions, dragons, and different serpents, all done in great detail with nothing missed. At the top of the four bedposts were four jewels, and they were far from small! They shone out, burning like the sun itself, and our hero, the noble Duke Ernst, thought that they were magnificent. There were two coverlets on the bed, both enclosed in very costly material indeed. There were silk bedsheets and covers made of ermine, with expensively made borders sewn with gemstones, and over everything was a silk bedspread with interwoven bands of gold thread and a border of fine braid. The two young warriors thought that this was amazing. Then they saw a massive and finely made chair next to the bed, decorated all over with carvings in pure white ivory picked out with gold—a veritable masterpiece. Four great amethysts, thick and as dark as blood, were set at the top of the back. A rich and expensive cloth lay across the seat, so that this chair stood ready by the magnificent bed. A square carpet of richly bordered blue velvet was spread on the floor. Two valuable gold goblets stood near to the bed, together with the finest wine in all that land, the best you could ever hope to drink. It was obvious from every detail that some careful and impressive preparations had been made.

When the two noble knights had inspected the rich trappings in this room and had left it again, they saw that right by it was a courtyard, long, broad, and well laid out, with many green cedar trees. They went farther in and found two springs flowing out of the courtyard, the one cold, the other warm. They had been so skillfully set up that they merged and flowed together, splashing into the same basin. Next to them was a fine bathhouse, covered over with green marble vaulting on strong buttresses—it could not have looked more beautiful! Two gleaming golden bathtubs stood there, with cleverly made silver pipes through which the water flowed into them. It was all so artfully constructed, that whether you wanted warm or cold water, pressure would allow the water through pipes to fill the tubs. It appears that an iron pipe on the far side of the bathhouse took the water farther, out into the whole citadel, which was excellent engineering. The streets, large and small, were paved with marble, some of them green as grass. If they felt in the citadel that it needed to be cleaned up, then the water could be channeled through the whole place, and dust and dirt would be washed away, and in a very short time it would be entirely cleaned. I cannot imagine that there is anywhere on earth a finer community. The streets gleamed like the snow.

When the bold Duke Ernst had seen all the wonders of this town, he said to Earl Wetzel: "My dear companion in arms, I should really like us to try out that bath! We needn't be afraid—as far as I can tell there isn't a single living thing here that could harm us while we are bathing. If anyone comes into this citadel we will very quickly be aware of it and can take measures to defend ourselves. We have suffered a lot without any respite while we were out on the wild ocean, so let us thank the Lord for bringing us here, where we can rest a little." The earl, his liegeman, replied: "If you insist upon that plan, then I shall have to go along with it, but you should know that if I had my way you would drop the idea. But since you won't take my advice," the brave knight went on, "then let us go quickly and take a brief bath. We must not forget that we are in a very odd situation here, and I am scared to death of being caught here unarmed."

Hurriedly the two bold warriors undressed and got into the bathtubs. They had to let the water fill the tubs, so they opened the taps on the silver pipes, and pure water flowed into the tubs, hot and cold mixed. It was very pleasant, and the two warriors enjoyed their bath. When they had finished, they left the bathhouse so that no one could attack them. Seeing no one, they hurried through the shining palace, went back to the chamber, and lay down to rest on the great bed with the fine decorations that they had seen before. A lot of people would have cause to regret this later on.

When the duke and his follower had rested for a while, Earl Wetzel said to his noble lord: "It is time for us to get up and go back to the ship and to the companions we left there. They are very likely to be worried about how we got on here in this citadel, and I am afraid that they will be pretty angry with us. Most noble lord, you should now get dressed, so that whatever happens to us we shall be prepared to defend ourselves. We have seen the great riches of this citadel, and we can say in all honesty that we have never seen anything, near or far, to match all this splendor. It is so extensive, so great, beautiful, and magnificent—completely admirable, in fact—that no other citadel anywhere in the world could be as fine, nor will anyone be able to build one like it in the future. I have to say that it is the crown of all cities that the world has ever known."

The two bold warriors delayed no longer and quickly armed themselves, and now looked and behaved like the fine fighters that they both were. Their weapons were splendid and admirable. There has never been an emperor, however great and powerful, whose forces they would not have graced, so fit and warlike did they now look. They took up their shields and hurried out of the chamber and through the glittering and shining palace. There were precious stones embellishing the vaulting, and the palace was beautifully decorated—what had been constructed here was an endless source of wonder. Such a magnificent hall has never seen the light of day anywhere in the whole world. [2207–2816]

They were still admiring all these marvels when they heard from the fields around the citadel a strange noise, strong and threatening, as if wild cranes had been gathered in one place, such was the unpleasant sound that they could now hear, a very loud and fearsome screaming noise. The two men were very surprised by this, and the bold warriors moved aside and took cover in a dark side room, where there was a window looking out over the gardens from above. They leaned out of this window, and without being seen themselves, they could see over the entire citadel, near and far, and what was going on inside and out in the fields. They now had to wait where they were. No one could get to them—they had chosen well and were concealing themselves carefully.

When the two brave warriors had been there for a little while and had kept watch everywhere, they suddenly saw a strange crowd of men and women at the gates of the citadel. Every one of them, young and old, was well shaped, with fine hands and feet, and was in every respect attractive and stately, except that their necks and heads were like those of a crane. They watched as a large number of these people rode toward the citadel. They had no other weapons than shields and bows, with well-made quivers—each of them had one—full of wicked-looking arrows. Their garments were made of rich materials, velvet and other costly stuffs, some tastefully decorated with silks and gold. There was not a single blemish on any of their bodies, except that their necks were too long—otherwise they looked like nobles. Men and women alike, they were all shapely, and clearly were people of power and strength.

I can tell you a little more of what I have heard about these strange people. They owned the citadel, in which they led bold and vigorous lives. They were proud, full of joie de vivre, very rich indeed, with as much gold and silver as anyone could desire, and they had many resources. They had a king, to whom the men and the women were all subject, and this king had traveled with his army across the sea in a fleet of ships, to the land of India. There he had killed their king just as he had been setting sail, with his wife, to visit one of his cities. He had been unable to defend himself and found himself in mortal danger, and the powerful king of Grippia struck him down at that moment and killed him. His ship, with the queen on board, had been sent to the bottom of the sea, and no one survived except the daughter of the king of India. Because of her great beauty, she alone was allowed to live, and all of the others who had been on the ship perished. The great king of Grippia wanted her as his wife and had joyfully brought her back to his home. All those splendid preparations had been for her benefit, and everyone—men, women, and children—had gone out happily to meet her when she had landed at the harbor and the citizens had heard of the arrival. These same strange people were now accompanying the bride with great clamor to the gates of the city, where men and women were waiting to receive her. Their clothing was especially finely made and attractively decorated. When our two brave warriors saw this amazing scene and had taken a good look at the strange people, they were not afraid of them and indeed were very dismissive of them.

Duke Ernst said to his companion, the earl: "I want us to stay here. Nothing can happen to us, and from here we can see everything that they do. We can also easily get away back to the ship whether they like it or not. It is still a long time till the evening, and we can easily stay here longer, until we have seen everything that they are going to do now. It is quite comical that their necks are so slender. I know that they will all go into the gardens, where the tables were set up and laid out with food. The meal was prepared for them this morning. They were clearly not worried about leaving everything and assumed that nothing whatever would happen to it—you see what I mean?"

"My lord, I am your liegeman," replied Earl Wetzel. "You can count on my loyalty, which I offer you gladly and happily with my life and my worldly goods. These people are not well armed against us, and even if there were more of them I should not be afraid of them. I could deal with a thousand or more of them on my own, and they would all suffer at my hand, if indeed they are even worthy as opponents. I could cut a pathway through them with my sword, and you can be sure that I would spare none of them. We are fully prepared to fight them, and if we keep well below their arrows, in a very short time we could kill so many that, unless I am much mistaken, they would have to abandon their bows, and this very day a good few of them would lose their heads. Things will not go well for them—their necks are so slender that plenty of heads will fall if they attack us. We shall show them here in their own fortress that they have never entertained such fierce guests in their land, and never will again."

And so they stayed. Then they saw two men walking together into the gates and noticed that they were wearing very rich garments, finely decorated with exotic silks. Over this they were wearing three-colored coats. Their breeches were cut in courtly fashion, and there were gold threads in their clothes. Their linen shone white as snow, and they both wore golden spurs. These two were of the highest-ranking aristocracy and thus were allowed to walk before the king. They walked elegantly and nobly, and their necks were slender and long, their heads exactly like those of cranes. In addition, each of them carried a fine quiver made of white ivory, with precious stones set around the top with the finest thread on expensive material. Each carried a bow fashioned from horn, with a silk bowstring. Their shields were beautifully made from gold, and where the boss should be there was a huge almandine garnet that could not have been more iridescent. Our two warriors had to acknowledge all this splendor.

Following these two they saw two more of them coming along, both dressed in cloaks of the finest velvet that you would ever find anywhere. Their inner garments were silk, sewn from head to toe with gold thread, studded with pearls. The many precious jewels that they wore shone beautifully, and their quivers and bows were equally magnificent. Each carried a shield with gold chasings that would be impossible to describe to you properly, and the same is true of the jewelry that they were wearing. Their noble bearing seemed entirely praiseworthy to our two warriors. For all that, these men were also like cranes. [2817–3056]

This group of four elegant aristocrats now entered the citadel. Following them was a fine, high-spirited man wearing dazzling garments. He wore the most expensive breeches, with gemstones and pearls, worked with gold all the way to his feet, on which he wore spurs of the finest red gold. His tunic was made of silk and his coat embroidered with gold from his throat down to his hands. All around the edges were magnificent wide braids. He wore a belt studded with gold, and the warriors saw that he was wearing a jeweled crown, which meant that he was the ruler of this country. His head and neck were shaped like those of a swan, hard though that is to believe. This was the king of Grippia. Two men walked behind him, also dressed more richly than you could find anywhere. These were of the highest nobility, and the king had chosen them to conduct between them the loveliest young woman ever born. Her skin was whiter than the snow, and greater beauty could not be imagined. Her hair reached nearly to the ground, and the young woman's body was covered with gold—no woman has ever been more finely dressed. But our warriors could see that she was walking along sadly, and she was weeping constantly. Her face, though, was that of a normal human being. A silken canopy under which the lady was walking gave her shade and relief from the heat, and four men carried it on finely worked red-gold staves. This most noble young woman had been born in India, and the king—as I have told you—had kidnapped her there. She was in a very sorrowful state, tortured by the misery of the death of her father and the fact that her mother had died with him. This would eventually lead to her own death.

Once she had been led in, a crowd of men and women thronged through the city gates until none of them, young or old, was left outside. In their own fashion they sang a wonderful-sounding song. They led the bride into a particularly fine room, and there was a great deal of noise as the festivities now began. There was plenty of room for the guests to sit at their ease. The king brought in the lovely young woman, and it was pitiful to see how she looked all around, and that no one said anything to her that she could understand. Everyone could see the tears from her eyes as they fell on her breasts. She was quite without any joy, and her clothing was dark as she stood there in great anguish.

However much these people might resemble humans, she could understand neither their speech nor their gestures. All she heard from men and women alike was the screeching of cranes, and I have absolutely no idea what they were saying. The lord chamberlain stood at the table and showed the honored guests where to sit, pointing to their seats with the staff that he held in his hand. He left no one standing, apart from those tasked with serving or pouring the wine. There was plenty of everything you could possibly desire.

And then the king of Grippia stepped forward in a dignified manner to take his place at table. The lovely young woman was seated by his side. She was so wretched that she looked completely out of place in all these celebrations. She and the king were given water in heavy golden bowls, and a number of the most important servants in magnificent court dress knelt and offered them the whitest of hand towels. Everyone behaved in an entirely courtly fashion where the king sat at table with his bride. Mead or wine was poured into all the golden goblets. There had been all kinds of food on silver dishes, but now the chamberlain discovered that it had been eaten. Everyone was very baffled as to how this might have come about. The chamberlain rapidly sent orders to the kitchens to have more food brought in, and plenty was supplied, so that people stopped wondering where the rest had gone. They assumed that their own people must have taken it and had no idea about the visitors, who were still not very far away. They might not have been invited, but they had still eaten the food and indeed enjoyed a bath, taking it all as a gift from heaven. But because of this a lot of people would die.

It was clear that there was plenty of mead and wine for everyone, and they soon brought out meat, cheese, and fish. Then they set up tables for the guests in the great hall. Water was passed around before they all went to take their places—there was not a single one of them who failed for any reason to wash his hands over a golden bowl. Once the assembly had all dried their hands, they moved solemnly toward the mighty king, where every one of them, whatever their status, bowed to him with great formality before they took their places. Footmen now took up their stations by the table. Never could a more magnificent meal be imagined. Game was served, and roast meat from farmed animals. All those gathered there ate and drank as much as they liked. Only the lovely young woman did not do so. She had no desire to eat, and she can hardly be blamed for not wanting to.

The king kissed her again and again by sticking his beak into her mouth, a kind of loving quite unknown to her while she lived in India. But now, in Grippia, she had to endure this form of love among these strange people. You could see that the bright eyes of the noble young woman were now dull and reddened, but there was no one to whom she could tell all her great woes. Duke Ernst now became aware of her tears and sorrows, however, and he and his companion, Earl Wetzel, were greatly saddened by the fact that the beautiful lady could find no one in that great throng to tell her troubles to. When the duke saw how miserable she was, he said to the earl: "If we cannot think of a way to get this lovely young woman away from here, then may I never enjoy anything in life again. I can see the misery of her situation, and it will be a sorrow to me forever. It pains my very heart that she has to suffer so much. My dear comrade in arms, we must think about how we can support her. If this beautiful young lady has to stay in this wretched place of exile until her dying day, it would be a very strange state of affairs. She doesn't know the language of these people and cannot understand them. If you agree, what I want us to do is to commit ourselves to God, and slip down and surprise them in the great hall with our swords ready. Before they can offer any resistance, we can spread so much death and confusion that they will never be able to cope with it. We can slaughter them like cattle before they know what is happening, and drench them in their own blood. All they have are their bows and arrows, and they will be no use against our ring-mail coats. We can press forward to where she is sitting next to the king and set her free from all her misery. We can kill the king and rescue her from her perilous situation—we shall carry the lovely lady away safely before they can put up any resistance. Even if they had a larger force, we could still get her to the city gates whether they like it or not. We shall have to use our swords to get us back to our companions unharmed. Well, my dear comrade, you must follow my plan so that we can move in quickly, as I said, because I am very sorry for that lovely young woman."

The earl replied: "Noble prince, take my advice and do not be in such a hurry. Of course I shall follow your orders, come what may. But you have seen for yourself how many people there are. We shall have to act with caution if we are to come out alive. If we attack while they are all still there, they will kill the lovely young woman, and we will not be able to prevent it. Rather than subject themselves to the shame of having her taken from them, they will find a way of killing her. We can help the lovely young woman better if we observe when they leave the table, because then the king will go with his guests into the hall, and his warriors will all leave the place. Then we can go into the room and kill the king immediately—he won't be able to escape—and if they try to stop us, we can cut a good many of them down. Then we can get the lady away from here. Before they know it, we shall be at the gates, and our companions will be able to come and give us powerful support. If I am any judge, we can then get across the open land, protecting the lady with our shields, and take her onto our ship."

The duke was pleased with this plan, and they did not have long to wait before the king had finished eating, and all those who had been sitting with him now stood up. The king went into the hall, and a throng of aristocratic-looking men gathered around him. Now there was dancing and singing—music was played for formal dances, and there was a great deal of shouting and screaming, which sounded like that of cranes or kites. This was in honor of the bride. Throughout the entire citadel the clamor was so loud that nothing like it had ever been heard before. When the people of Grippia played all kinds of strange games in front of the bride, this did not help her to feel any better, however close she sat to the king, so profound was her misery, and this began to irritate the mighty king. He at once ordered the crowds to leave, and wanted to withdraw into their chamber. Those assigned to the task now conducted the lady into the finely appointed room, and the great noise of singing all around the place accompanied them. All the people who had been with them now dispersed and went off—as is usual—to their own lodgings; and they could not have foreseen the damage that they were to suffer later on. They went off home now to take their ease, but trouble would follow them. [3057–3400]

The people, men and women alike, had all left when they had been dismissed, and no one remained except twelve of the highest-ranking nobles, whom the king always kept by him as his counselors and advisers. They had gone into the chamber and were about to disrobe the bride when one of the king's people came over to the dark area and saw the two fully armed warriors. As soon as he spotted them, he rushed back to the room and shouted out that he had seen two men. The people of Grippia assumed that they were enemies who had followed them back from India to attack them. They were completely shocked by this and immediately attacked the beautiful young woman in revenge. They stabbed her repeatedly all over her body with their beaks, and the noble lady screamed loudly.

The two warriors were startled and angry, and the duke and his companion began to regret their action. Ernst said: "We held back for too long, and her screams mean she is in terrible danger. They have killed the lady in that chamber, and now they shall suffer swift vengeance." The two warriors rushed toward the chamber, drawing their glittering blades as they did so. They hacked down the king and his men with their swords, and those who were in the chamber fell at their hands. All lay dead but one, the man who had first spotted them, and who had narrowly managed to escape as soon as he had heard the clash of swords. He dodged behind Ernst and Wetzel and hurtled through the door without stopping to bid them farewell, and so just got away with his life. Having escaped from the bridal chamber, this man now spread the news in the whole city, and the citizens raised a great clamor.

Duke Ernst bent over the lady and spoke to the lovely woman. "I am sorrier than I can say that you may lose your dear life," he said, "and in my heart I shall never cease from weeping for you. By God, those that did this to you shall pay for it. Tell me now, lovely lady, if you can be saved! If by God's grace you can be healed, then you need have no doubt that I and the many warriors I have on my ship will take you back to your home. But most noble lady, if you should die, I shall take vengeance on your enemies right now, so that they suffer for it for the rest of their lives. This very day we exiles and wanderers will give them, before we travel on, a punishment so great that they and their descendants will always have cause to remember it with pain."

The daughter of the king of India lay there in misery and agony. She could do nothing, and death was fast approaching as the girl lay there soaked in warm red blood. Things could not have been worse, as she was racked with great pain, and her heart was breaking in her body. The most noble lady grew weaker and weaker, and she said to Duke Ernst: "May God reward you for the brave efforts you have made in the face of danger, most worthy knight, to help me in this foreign land. Whatever happens to me, I shall thank God for giving me the comfort of your aid, and that you, sir, have set me free from the continued miseries I would always have had to suffer in this marriage. If by the grace of God I really were to survive this and go on living, then you would have good cause for rejoicing. If with the help of Our Lord you could bring me back to India, and if you wished to stay there, I would make you, most brave and noble warrior, very rich and powerful, so that you would be the equal of kings. Your power would be so great that you would be a sovereign and would enjoy all kinds of pastimes and pleasures. You would rule over many wealthy lands, and they would be yours, as I said. My father had command over many fierce warriors. All his aristocrats, dukes, and earls served him faithfully and with honor. Wherever he led them, they supported him in times of war, and for that he rewarded them with red gold. He was justly acclaimed by everyone as long as he lived. But then came disaster when the king of Grippia attacked us with his men. He came to us by sea and took the lives of my father, my dear mother, and the whole retinue that had been on their ship. None of them, nobles or commoners, survived, except myself alone, and they brought me here. I am my father's only child, and you should know that when he was killed, no one but I had the right to bear the crown. Sadly, things have turned out differently. I will have to stay in this foreign land until Judgment Day because I can live no longer. But I prefer death to having to endure those miseries for my whole life. May God grant you the good fortune of being able to get safely back to your homeland." She inclined her head to the warrior, unable to speak any more, and with her last breath her soul left her body. [3401–3576]

The duke and his companion were greatly affected by the fate of the lovely girl, and both wept in sorrow and misery, so great was the pain caused by her death. They placed the beautiful young woman on a bier and spread a fine gold cloth over her and prayed that the Lord God, creator of all things, should through His grace be merciful to her. In great sadness the two warriors left the chamber in which the terrible events had taken place, left the palace, and made for the gates of the citadel. They held their shields in front of them as if seeking battle. They were keen to gain renown with their sharp swords, or to die for the sake of the beautiful lady. Protected by their shields, then, the noble warriors moved forward.

Now, however, the city gates were blocked with men on both sides, since the people of Grippia had surrounded them. The streets of the city were full of men, and they made a fearsome noise as they came toward the two fighters, who were unable to get out of the city. They had to hack a pathway through them with their swords, and amazing deeds were carried out against the strange people of Grippia. The two knights offered their fighters a grim repayment. They held their shields boldly before them, and then the brave warriors rushed with all their strength at the crowd. Many a furious blow was struck, and their swords could not miss those long, thin necks. It was hard to believe how many of them were cut down. Hardly any of them escaped with their lives, whichever way they turned, and the two warriors made it clear that they were not inclined to spare anyone who fought against them, so that great numbers of them died. Many of those who perished were considered to be worthy opponents. The two men carved a passage almost to the gates, and many more fell before they could get through. The city gates were closed and bolted, and the two indomitable fighters had to face more great attacks, and many more were killed.

Now the worthy warriors took up a position with their backs to a wall, fighting for their lives. Both men had to defend themselves from attacks from the front and the side, and in a short time many of their adversaries came to rue the day. They were assailed on all sides with bows and arrows, which were the enemies' sole weapon of attack, and their shields were so stuck with arrows that they could scarcely hold them up. They slashed them off with their swords and trampled on them, defending themselves that way and killing very many, but they were in great peril and were afraid they might not come out alive. By now, though, their companions on the ship had become aware of the battle, and these bold warriors came to their aid with sharp and heavy swords, following their war banner to the city gates. Without any delay they hacked open the gates themselves and forced their way well into the citadel at sword point. This was vital for the duke and the earl, because otherwise they would have died. But help and support came, and they were saved.

In the storm of battle many warriors lost their lives. They had to escape from those defending the battlements, who were hurling down a rain of stones. The duke and his followers could not safely stay there any longer, so they made efforts to get away without losses. The rest and the bath had cost the two warriors dearly. Now the brave fighters were compelled—though still in good spirits—to return with the men to their ship, and put out to sea. The duke and his men were, however, faced with a surprise that would put them in dire peril, because as the brave men were about to reach the ship something happened that would cost the lives of many of them. [3577–3704]

As I have said, the duke had escaped from the city unscathed, and the bold young warrior was heading for his ship, wanting to get his men out to sea again. Then suddenly they saw a great army of the lords of that land, knights who had wanted to come and see the king's bride. Our Christian warriors thought that there must have been twelve thousand or more, all richly and powerfully armed, and they saw them riding toward them on the finest battle-chargers that the world has ever seen. They had bows made of horn, and their quivers and shields were exotically patterned, and there was a great horde of them. When our brave fighters were trying to get to their ship they saw these riders coming at them and began a bitter fight in which many lives were lost.

When the noble duke saw this army coming at them, he said to his men: "What do you think, my friends? Today you can show your daring in battle. We shall meet them in battle like brave knights. Now that they have cut off our way back to the ship, you must rally around our standard and put up a valiant defense. We can earn admission to paradise with our lives. The honor of reaching heaven has to be earned, but there we shall have unalloyed joy everlasting. Let us earn that today. Our enemies are not baptized and are strangers to God. If it is not the Lord's will that we are killed here, then all they can do is drive us down to the sea. They have a strong army, and we have no choices. You should all turn your hearts to Our Lord, that He may be merciful to us and help us in this hour of need. My warriors, do not fear death. We set out in the name of God, and if our lives are taken from us in this place, we are still saved. Be ever more resolute, then, and fight fiercely for the grace of God, who has so often given us His aid and taken away our fears. When they get close enough to us that we can reach them, as long as we can hold a sword we shall cut down so many that they will not be able to mourn them all."

After the noble warrior had rallied his men, they did not hesitate but prepared themselves for battle, as brave fighters must. The duke himself grasped the standard and led his men out. Many of the fast battle-chargers came riding at him, and the enemy began the battle. Great numbers of them drew their strong bows and sent arrows flying at them from a long way away. Shields and hauberks offered little protection, and they bore down on the noble duke in great numbers, still firing arrows from a distance. Their shields did offer some defense, but they were surrounded on the broad plain, and unfortunately they were unable to reach the enemy with their swords. They kept back the heathen fighters who were pressing in on them, but they could not inflict any damage on them because they kept moving. With their fast warhorses they did not come close enough to allow those steeds to be caught. The bold duke was greatly disturbed by this, and it seemed wrong that the enemy would not fight in close combat on foot. Ernst's men suffered losses and setbacks.

When the duke realized that their defense was not working, he took up the standard and forced a path through the strong enemy army down to the sea and to his ship. To do this the noble warrior had to withstand fighting and great danger, and five hundred of his men were either killed or wounded. He helped those who survived—as a true hero must—and eventually the fine warrior reached the seashore, protected by his shield. The earl stood firm by his side as close comrades always do, and ordered all his men to get to the ship as quickly as possible to save their lives. The warriors kept the enemy at bay long enough for the sailors to get to shore with their boats and take them across to the ship. When they got there, Ernst and Wetzel leaped onto the ship, and they set sail. The Good Lord at once sent them the best possible wind—better than anyone could ever had wanted—and thus they were relieved of many of their sorrows, and their spirits were revived. They put on full sail and traveled across the unknown ocean. But still they were deeply saddened by the companions that they had had to leave behind.

Now the wind took them far out over the sea, but their heathen enemies were so angry with them over their own losses that it was not long before they tried to pursue the poor exiles in fast galleys. They wanted to make sure that the exiles did not escape alive. The duke and his men, all noble and worthy knights, got away very quickly and were soon out of their sight, so that the pursuers could not find them and rapidly turned back. When the people of Grippia heard that the king and many of his men had been killed and were lying dead, they set up a great cry of mourning after they had found them. Then they carried the dead away and quickly buried them, and called in physicians to tend to the wounded. They soon chose a new ruler, having lost their former king when death had carried him off.

Ernst and his men, thanks be to God, had sailed away. [3705–3882]

CHAPTER 5

A PERILOUS JOURNEY

The duke and his companions, the noble pilgrims, were sailing into the jaws of death and would face many tribulations on the face of the ocean, but—as I shall now tell you—many of their sins were washed away.

It is said that on the twelfth day they came very close to land, where the warriors saw a high mountain in the sea, and their ship made for it. This place was called Magnet Rock. As you may imagine, they were very pleased to come in sight of it. Then they saw the masts of many ships, as thick as a forest. The bold warriors were delighted by this and believed that all their troubles would now be over. They imagined that they would find cities and people in that country, just as they had in Grippia. They were still a good way off, however. As I have said, they saw the masts towering up over the ships, but they were white as snow, bleached by the wind and weather, stripped and bare.

The warriors did not hesitate but sailed cheerfully onward on these unknown seas, the good men thinking that all would be well. But then one of the crew climbed to the crow's nest while the current was pulling them strongly toward the harbor. The sailor was shocked when he recognized the mountain, and in fear and horror he called down to the warriors on the ship.

"Most noble fighters, prepare yourselves for eternity! We are lost, and we shall have to stay here forever. That great rock in front of us is in the Sea of No Return, and unless God saves us, we shall all die here. We are being driven onto the rocks, and I have heard tales about them. In true penitence you should turn to God and repent in your hearts of any wrongs you have done. Warriors, I shall tell you about the power of these rocks and what they can do. Any ship that sails within thirty miles of them will quickly be pulled toward them—yes, it is true. If it has iron rivets, a ship will be pulled there helplessly. We saw the ships there beneath the dark mountain, and there we shall die of starvation. There is nothing we can do—the same thing has happened to all those who have sailed here. Pray now to God for His mercy and His help. We are very close to the rocks!"

When the duke heard that, the noble leader said to his warriors: "My dear comrades-in-arms, we now have to implore the Lord above that He might receive us through His grace into his heavenly kingdom. We may well perish on these rocks. Now let us praise God with our hearts and voices. If we should die on these unknown seas, all will still be well if we may be with God in the kingdom of heaven. So let us all rejoice that we are so close to the Lord." When the men heard this, they took it to heart and followed their leader's advice by turning all their thoughts and efforts toward God and His commandments, with confessions and penance and the proper fear that is due to the Lord. Thus they prepared their souls well.

Once the exiled travelers had said their prayers and put their affairs in order, they cried out pitifully to God, imploring their creator that He might preserve their souls. By now they were very near to the rocks, and they could clearly see the ships with the high masts. The rocks pulled the warriors toward them with great speed, pulling so powerfully that this ship would outrun any other. It ran with such force toward the rocks that all the ships crashed against one another. The masts banged together and the collisions were so strong that many ships were broken apart. A large number of travelers had been received in this fashion and had later perished, so that they never returned. It may be deemed a miracle that none of the men was struck down and killed by one of the old and rotting masts falling hard upon their ship from the others. If one of these fell, nothing that was anywhere near could withstand it. It was a great wonder that our men and their ship survived, and that all the debris fell into the sea. Now the duke and his followers had to cope with great dangers, faced as they were with grim death itself. Nevertheless, the brave men made it alive onto the rocks—a clear sign of divine assistance.

When the ship hit the rocks, the warriors did what everyone does who has been in one place for a long time and wanted to disembark—the bold knights jumped off at once and went to look at the amazing sight of all the other ships, close by one another like trees in a forest on the sea surrounding the mountain. Neither before nor since has anyone ever seen such riches as our bold warriors found on these ships, so much so that it was a long time before they could take account of it all and grasp what it all was. All around lay silver, gold, jewels, purple cloth, velvet, and shining silks, more than anyone could reckon. [3883–4068]

When they had inspected these amazing things, they moved on. The duke and his men climbed the mountain to find out if they could see any land from there, but none of them could spy out anywhere else where they might reach land. This troubled them a great deal. The mountain stood alone in the wide ocean, and here the helpless warriors could perish and die of starvation, a thought that lay heavy upon them. Now the famed heroes were prey to great fears, but they all agreed that they would suffer things bravely, since Almighty God had imposed this suffering upon them, as He had upon all those who had come there before them and had ended their lives in that place. Since they could not avoid their fate, they would suffer death for the grace of God and would accept this terrible situation as a penance for their sins. The duke and his companions still put their trust in the one born of the Blessed Virgin. The travelers lived on the ship and endured such suffering as they had never before experienced in their lives, because they used up the supplies of good food that they had brought from Grippia, where the warriors had obtained it so boldly. All those on the ship died of starvation, so that none of them survived of the whole company except the duke himself and with him another six men. When the other men died, they were carried off one at a time by a griffin. As far as the survivors were concerned, when one of the men was near death, the bold warriors carried him up from below and laid him on the deck of the ship—there have been plenty of reports of this kind of thing—and the griffins flew down and carried him off to their nest. And it was in this way that the duke and his remaining men were helped by the griffins to get away. The others were eaten by the griffins and their young. They had often managed to do this, and many people had been carried off to their nests; it was in this manner that the bold warriors, the duke and his companions, would manage to get back to the mainland.

The duke was greatly distressed to see his shipmates tormented by hunger and starving to death while he was unable to help them, and he suffered miserably each time death took one of his men away, until there were only seven of the brave warriors left. Even these were barely surviving the pains of hunger. All they had left was half a loaf, which they divided among themselves—wretched though that was, they had nothing else—and they commended themselves body and soul to the power of God. The bold warriors knelt in the form of a cross and prayed fervently to Our Lord that He might have mercy upon them and grant them aid in necessity. They were very afraid of death.

When these poor souls had finished their prayers (which would indeed help them later), Earl Wetzel said: "I have been thinking of a plan that could be the best chance for us. If we are going to survive, I am certain that what we must do is make a thorough search in the ships to find some animal hides and cover ourselves with them—poor exiles that we are—putting them on top of our armor. Once we have been sewn into the skins," the earl went on, "then we should lie down at the front of the ship. The griffins will pick us up and carry us away, but they will not be able to hurt us because of the armor that has preserved us so often before. When we see that the older griffins want to feed their young, then we will cut ourselves out and get back down to the ground. At all events, if a different fate is still determined for us, and God does not want us to survive, then it will be much better to die bravely in action than to go on suffering so miserably here."

The men said that God must have inspired him with this plan, and they hurried down to the ships, where they found a large number of sea-cow hides. The warriors were very encouraged by this and went happily back to their own ship. They cut one of the hides into strips to use for sewing themselves in, and that night they prepared everything else they needed for this venture. They undertook this great effort full of trust in Our Lord, who had saved them so often before.

When everything that they needed for this new journey was ready, they debated among themselves who should be the first to be sewn into the animal hide. Earl Wetzel declared that: "It should be my lord duke and myself. I shall sew us both into two hides, because I do not propose to be parted from him, dead or alive. I shall suffer with him all fears and dangers, whatever the outcome. Whatever happens in this undertaking, whether we survive or whether we die, or if we perish in some other way, then it has to happen to both of us together. You should all be aware that if God permits us to go on living and to escape from the young griffins, then you, too, will soon be carried away from here. Don't weep for us! No one can tell just how strong these birds are. But if we survive, we shall all meet again." And that is what did eventually happen.

This was thought to be good, and the two men prepared themselves at daybreak. They quickly put on the good armor that every warrior has who needs to go into battle properly armed—helmet, shield, and iron greaves. They did not put their swords in their sword belts but took them along, the bare blades by their sides. Then they were sewn into the sea-cow hides. Their companions wept when they had to carry them out. The duke then told his men to have faith in God and act accordingly. They should sew each other into the strong animal hides, and they should then trust to God to look after them. The men all wept bitterly for the noble duke. Parting was painful, but they followed his instructions.

When it was fully daylight, they lifted up their leader, as has been described, and laid him down on the ship's deck, firmly wrapped in the strong animal hides. As they always did, the griffins now came flying across the broad ocean toward the ships. When they saw the hides, they each took one in their talons, gripping them very firmly and taking them back to their young, dropping them into their nest in front of them. The young griffins tried, but they could not get at their food in any way, nor could they tear into the hides, and simply had to leave them where they were. The two men cut themselves out and climbed down over cliffs into the forest, where the griffins could not harm the brave warriors. In His great mercy, God had saved them from terrible danger, and they gave thanks to the Lord, their creator.

These two were now safe, and, free of all fear, they now hid in the thick forest. Meanwhile, the griffins had flown back and fetched two more men. Once these had been brought across the sea to the nest, the same thing happened as before—they cut themselves free and climbed down, escaping from the young griffins. The adult griffins then flew off a third time and without much delay and got two more of the men who had been sewn into the hides, but a third man was too weak to defend himself, and he died in the sea. The other two had again been carried off as food for the young griffins, who tried to get at them from all sides with their sharp talons, but they were forced to let our travelers live. These men did as the others had done, and climbed down into the forest. Duke Ernst, the brave and noble warrior, was pleased when he saw them coming to him, and with delight he hurried to meet them and embraced each one of them. God had worked a miracle, as so often before, and the warriors were relieved that it was the will of God that they should overcome their misfortune. Now that they all had come together again, they were overjoyed that once again Our Lord in His great mercy had restored them to life. The duke and his men had rightly taken care not to kill the young griffins, because if they had done so, the adult griffins would not have carried away any more of them, because they were taking them for their young. The lives of all the men had been saved, however. [4069–4349]

They now set off through the forest, and the bold warriors were in good spirits, although they could not find any proper food there but ate roots and plants and anything else they could find. Eventually, the poor pilgrims reached a wide and fast-flowing river, which was nevertheless clear and looked good. The wanderers' spirits lifted when they saw it, and they were able to rest and eat there, because it was full of fish. The noble knights went into the water and caught enough fish with their bare hands to be able to feed themselves and stave off the hunger. Again they gave thanks to God. They were able to light a fire and could grill the fish on it. After that the bold warriors searched up- and downriver to see if there was a place where they could cross, but they were soon disappointed and had to turn back. Upriver there was a rocky gorge, and downriver mountains that reached to the sky; the river ran through them, broad and with an indescribably strong current. The men bewailed their journey into exile and thought once more that they had reached the end.

Once again they called out to God in their distress, fearing that it would be their death if they could not get across. As you have heard, the river was broad and deep, and they were going to have to face further tribulations, about which they were very fearful. The river flowed swiftly into the mountain by way of a narrow tunnel, through rock-strewn rapids.

"We have to consider," said the bold duke, "what we should do next. We shall die if we stay here for much longer." The loyal Earl Wetzel said: "It looks hopeless. Since we can't cross the river, we have to take a great risk. Let us without delay build a raft large enough and strong enough to save our lives. We shall have to go through that tunnel in the rocks. There's no other way, and God will decide if we live or die."

They all set to at once and quickly made a large and strong raft. They brought together great tree trunks that they had hacked down with their swords, because they had no other tools. They bound them with supple willow and then carefully boarded their raft, committing themselves devotedly to Our Lord and His Blessed Mother and all of His saints, and genuflected toward heaven before they let themselves be carried into the tunnel.

The amazing feats of these warriors and what happened to them are still spoken about to this very day. They had plenty of problems even before they got through—the raft had to withstand many great blows from the rocks, and they were in constant fear until they got to the other side of the mountain. Often the crash of their raft against rocks might have been fatal, but Our Lord and Savior protected them in their hour of need.

They suffered a great deal, nevertheless, before they made it through the pitch-dark tunnel, as their craft was battered right and left. There inside the mountain all kinds of stones shone, beautiful and of many different colors, and the riverbed beneath them shone as well. Ernst, the noble warrior, noticed among the shining stones one gem that he broke off from the rocky wall. The noble duke took this gem, which shone with special beauty, with him out of this dangerous situation. Because of its splendor it is called "the Orphan Stone," and it is still well known to us—you can see it in the imperial crown, and its presence there proves the truth of this story. If there should be anyone who is still inclined to think that this tale is all lies, then let him come to Bamberg, and he will certainly have his views rebutted by the master who made this story. It was composed in Latin, and it is without any doubt a true story. [4350–4476]

CHAPTER 6

A NEW KING AND NEW CHALLENGES

When the men saw daylight again, the walls began to widen, and before too long they came out into a broad plain. The duke and his companions were delighted and steered to the bank, where they left their raft. The bold and valiant warriors soon came to a thick wood, where they found a group of forest dwellers, whose language they did not understand. They ran toward them, but when the others saw the travelers they fled, men, women, and children alike. The warriors found enough bread, however, to feed themselves and stave off hunger, because they had again been weakened. They set off farther into the forest, and God brought them to a very fine land. It was a kingdom in which they could see a number of fine citadels, and we are given to understand that the name of this country was Arimaspi. The duke was very pleased indeed to be there, now that the warriors had arrived in the territory of an important ruler who had built a magnificent citadel. You should know that it was large and strong-looking. The people who lived there, however, were unusual, and it cannot be denied that they looked quite fearsome. They only had one eye, in the middle of the forehead, and are called "Circle-Eyes," or cyclops in Latin.

By now the warriors had come closer to the strongly built citadel and were very anxious about how they would be received here, how they would manage, and what would happen next.

The duke said, "We shall go there trusting in the mercy of God," and they soon became aware of the lord of that city taking his ease with his knights by the gates. This lord received the men courteously and with honor and conducted them to a richly appointed palace. Their host was very friendly toward them, although they did not understand his language. The lord of the city indicated with gestures that they could take off their armor. Things were going well.

This lord was a good host. He treated his guests courteously and offered them what the knights greatly needed; namely, all kinds of food and clothing, and all to their tastes. The lord ordered them to be given clothing made of expensive materials. He was himself very well bred and recognized by their demeanor that these were also noblemen, which made him sympathetic to their plight, and he looked after them for a long time. It then happened that there was a great festival, and the king of that country sent word out to all his relatives and supporters that they should not fail to attend at court. So now the princes from far and wide in that empire assembled there, and all the nobles from near or far came to the court. The lord of this city also went to the court with great ceremony. He took with him to the king the duke and his companions, all appropriately armed, with gleaming hauberks and iron greaves. They were very impressive in their shining armor, and when the king saw them he greeted them one by one and was greatly impressed by them. He asked the nobleman where these knights had come from or where he had found them, and he replied: "Your majesty, I do not know where they come from or who they are. They came to my castle, but I do not know where from, though they were wretched-looking and starving. I told my people," he said, "to feed and care for them, as you can see. They do not understand our language, but their bearing is noble."

The powerful king looked at their helmets, shields, and swords, and the men seemed to him to be fine and worthy. Their demeanor pleased him, and he asked the lord to give them to him, so they were passed on to the king. The king was delighted with this outcome. He was interested in these warriors, and he quickly ordered that an especially fine, handsome, and strong Castilian stallion be brought to them in the courtyard. He wanted to find out this way who was the most important of the men. Ernst, the renowned hero, at once grasped the reins and sprang without stirrups onto the horse and rode as a true horseman. With this, the great king took Ernst and all his men into his service and made sure they were excellently equipped. He appointed a chamberlain to attend to their needs, and he instructed his own people to serve them in any way they desired. This was done willingly, and thus God had again looked after the men.

So now they stayed with the king. Once the court festival was over, the king spent many a day with them, and it is true to say that they were well looked after for a whole year, until they had learned the language. A short while later the king summoned the duke and asked him politely to tell him the whole story of what land they had come from and what his name was, and also to tell him in all truth which ruler he served, and how he came to be in that country. The warrior answered him and told him the whole story, that he had been a duke in his homeland, and how through no fault and with no shame of his own he had been driven out by the mightiest ruler that there had ever been in that empire from its very beginnings. He explained in detail the customs and nature of his homeland, and how they had come to this kingdom. When the king had heard the whole story of how he came to be there, about what had happened in the many lands he had been in and the troubles he had had to face there since he had left his own country, he gave orders to all of his people that they should make every effort to look after these men well. He laid great emphasis on this and was from then on bound in friendship to the duke. He gave him gold and silver and anything else he wished for. This was all by the grace of God. [4477–4666]

But we can leave all that, because I want to go on with the story.

Near to the country of the king of Arimaspi lived a curious race of people who were known as sciapods, and they were wreaking havoc in his lands and causing a great deal of damage. Sciapods have very broad feet, rather like those of a swan, and they are very strong indeed, which means that they are able to cross otherwise difficult terrain like brushland or scrub, and all without shoes. If they were caught in storms without any shelter, they would simply lie on the ground and cover themselves with one foot (strange but true!), and if the storm went on for a long time, they changed feet when the first foot became tired. The point is that they were protected at all times, with no need to worry about any weather conditions.

These sciapods had declared war on the king of Arimaspi. They were an arrogant people, and their weapons—which fired bolts—were terrifying. In the course of a day and a night they had gathered and mobilized a large army to attack the king's lands, and what they had in mind was a slash-and-burn onslaught on the king and his lands, to lay waste to his entire state.

Reports came to the king that the sciapods had already forced their way across his borders, and he was horrified when he heard this terrible news. The king was able in a few short days to raise a great army of the very bravest of fighters, however, and they mustered on a very broad and open plain and set up camp there. This was going to be the place where battle between the two armies would have to decide who would live and who would die. In fact, the sciapods had brought their weapons for nothing, because once Duke Ernst entered the battle, they were not given a chance to use them. He took over command and led the vanguard himself under the king's flag. The sciapods fought against him with great boldness, and a great horde of them threw themselves upon his men, starting a battle in which a great many men would die.

Ernst and his men held fast against them, cutting and thrusting at the enemy until they were able to break through their line. At this the enemy had to give way to him, after which they were cut down savagely where they stood, until the paths through the battlefield itself were strewn with the dead. The king of Arimaspi gave the duke full support with his troops, and they defeated the sciapods so thoroughly that hardly any of them escaped alive. It was the duke's victory and triumph, and he and his men had killed unimaginable numbers of the enemy.

The battle had been won. Those who did manage to get away fled either back to their own towns or to the forests, or wherever they were able to find refuge of some sort. The king stayed triumphant on the battlefield that night, and there were noisy celebrations that went on until the next morning. The king then wanted to reward all of the men, so he summoned his trusted lieutenants to come to him and commanded them to thank the duke for the faithful assistance he had given him in maintaining his honor. He praised him greatly for his bravery and said: "Most noble young sir, you have upheld my honor and preserved my life in a valiant and vigorous fashion, so that from henceforth you shall rule as much of my lands as you wish. Out of the love and gratitude that I feel for you, I intend to give you so much land that you will yourself be able to enjoy power, fame, and the esteem of others." He rewarded the warrior by conferring upon Ernst a dukedom of Arimaspi, with its accompanying vassals and lands. Then, before they parted, he loaded Ernst's men with many gifts for themselves. Earl Wetzel, the duke's second-in-command, was immediately placed in charge of the new duchy and of the people, rich or poor, something that was formally accepted, and the king then rode off to Lucerna, which was the name of his city. The duke and his men were taken to his new lands. Things had turned out very well for him. [4667–4790]

Once the duke had gained his new territory, he won over his vassals, so that they served him happily and willingly. He gave them gold and silver and was generous to all, and what he gave was always welcome. Because of this, the most noble duke could not fail to be liked by his subjects. He always behaved honorably, faithfully, and thoughtfully. He stood by them through good times and bad, and Earl Wetzel, too, carried out his offices with honor. The two of them were reckoned to be the best rulers that could be found in any lands, near or far. They were held in great esteem.

The story tells us further that the noble Duke Ernst heard reports of another very unusual race, who lived on a plain by the sea and were very foolhardy. They were able to call together a large force when they wanted to, and they were once again rather odd to look at. They were well built and not weaklings, but their ears were so long that they reached down to their feet, and they could wrap them around their bodies. It is said that they wore no other clothes. They could fight well, and they were like regular warriors. Later, many of them would be defeated by the duke's army. They carried sharp javelins, well made and bright, and they were a match for anyone. They were sworn enemies of the king of Arimaspi and had often attacked him and caused a lot of harm. Thus far, the people in that country had suffered their attacks, but now they begged the duke to change the situation.

When Ernst was informed about this, the noble duke at once sent for his warriors and gathered together a sound army to use against these people. He went down to the sea and found out how to get to their territory. Meantime, however, the panotii, these long-eared people, had also armed themselves well. They were eager to join battle with the duke, and there was no delay—they rushed at him from a distance, something they would pay for when it came to fighting. The duke's men inflicted deep wounds on them with their swords, and those that did not manage to run away were immediately killed, until the greater part of their forces lay dead or seriously wounded. The battle went on into the night, but the duke was victorious. His men were greatly pleased, and the duke stayed triumphant on the battlefield that night. At daybreak they saw many men lying there in their own blood, and there had been losses among the warriors on both sides. The duke, however, would not leave until he and his forces had conquered all the people of this land, however long it might take for them to give in and become his subjects, providing him with men when he wanted to travel over the seas. For now, he led his army back to his own lands. He had lost some of his warriors, but he had had the good fortune to be victorious in every battle. [4791–4890]

He was happy to return to his castle, and he arranged for a great feast for his knights and gave them gifts of gold and clothing. He now heard that not far away there was a country called the Land of the Pygmies. The people who lived there were very small indeed, tinier than could be imagined. It was a kingdom, but the people lived in fear, and I shall tell you why. The country was full of cranes, who had taken over the land so that the people no longer dared to go out into the fields. They had to live in dense forests where these tiny people could, with difficulty, escape from the birds. I should say that they lived off the eggs that they regularly stole from the cranes, as many as they could. They also took young cranes if they found them, but this was their only food apart from what they could grow in the forest. They had no other means of survival, because they were defenseless against the cranes and would have needed to call upon an army to attack them. Any of the cranes that they managed to kill or capture were then divided up equally among them all, rich or poor, until the next time they caught one.

When the duke heard this story, he called together a hundred knights, and they set off by ship to that country. When the warriors arrived there, they went into the dense forest to assess the situation and see what state the people were in, and there they found many of them in one place. The duke asked which of them was the king and then promised them that they need fear no longer—"I swear this on my honor!"

A NEW KING AND NEW CHALLENGES

The people were delighted and took him to their ruler, who embraced every one of them in greeting and received every single one, whoever they were, with great courtesy—of that you can be sure. The king himself barely reached the duke's waist. Ernst asked him to take them to where they could see the dangerous birds. The king, however, had before this sent out to summon the people in his kingdom, and they came at once and showed Ernst the place, as he had asked. They found an unbelievably vast number of the birds, too many to be counted.

The cranes did not flee from the army but defended themselves boldly. They were belligerent and not inclined to fly away, and they were fiercely attacked by the king's men and his guests, and so many cranes were killed that I can truly say that no one, man or woman, could tell you the exact but astoundingly large number. Vengeance had been taken. The men stayed for six weeks in that country because the king had requested that they remain and help him drive away the cranes from his country altogether, and the warriors killed all those who had been oppressing the people. The noble duke's military intervention was of great benefit to the people of that land. The king summoned the duke and asked the great hero to stay there forever. He wanted him to take over his own status as ruler and was more than ready to become his vassal. The duke said, however: "My lord, I cannot accept. May God ever protect and keep your land for you. I cannot stay, because I have to return to my own country. You can, however, do me the honor of letting some of your people come with me. Know this, my lord: for as long as I live I shall always be ready to serve you."

The king replied, "You may take as many as you like." The noble duke selected, with the advice of his men, two of them who were strong, well built, and behaved with dignity. Before he left, the king again thanked him for his help and for the honor he had shown them, and then the duke took his leave and returned home in good spirits to the land of Arimaspi, giving thanks to Almighty God. [4891–5012]

Not too distant from the land of Arimaspi there lived a fearsome race called the Anakim of Canaan, mighty warriors known also as Gigantes. They had subjugated many other countries, who now had to pay tribute to them, and many a brave knight had been robbed of his life and found death at their hands, because if anyone refused to pay tribute, their lives were forfeit. The king of the Anakim was advised by his men to send to Arimaspi and give their king this ultimatum: that if he valued his life and wanted to stay in his own country, then he should send a tribute and afterward come in person to receive his land back as a fief, accepting immediate subjugation to them as a vassal. There could be no question of negotiation, because it was bad enough that they had been independent for so long.

The envoy was a powerful giant who came to Arimaspi and presented his lord's message formally to the king. The king of Arimaspi was afraid that there would be great suffering if the giants invaded their land. He might not be able to offer a defense, nor even save himself unless he ran away, and he and his land might only survive at all if the giants allowed them to do so. The king therefore sent for the best men that he had, and they came together as a war council, Duke Ernst among them. The king gave them a detailed report of the giants' message. "They are so powerful that no one can withstand them. I am very concerned."

All of his men advised him that since they could think of nothing else, the best he could do would be to send the tribute so that they could stay at peace in their own country. Duke Ernst, however, said to them: "Your advice does you no honor at all, suggesting to your king such a shameful course of action for your country! In my country no one would advise anyone to subjugate himself to someone of equal status. I will give you better counsel. Reply to the king of the giants that he is too lowborn for you to receive your own country as a fief from his hand. Say that it is madness on his part, and if he has any concern for decency and honor, he should never make such a suggestion again. You would dishonor yourselves to agree! Tell him that if he were nevertheless to attack your lands, that you would then defend it so strongly that he would not like that tribute at all, and that any tribute and payment he took away from here would be very painful to him indeed!"

The king was very pleased to hear this, sent for the envoy, and gave him the gifts appropriate to his office, and then said: "You may return home and tell your lord that his attitude to me should be of a more friendly nature. It is a very foolish idea indeed to try to get payment from me, and he should not concern himself quite so much with silver and gold. If he behaves amicably toward me, then I shall gladly reciprocate. But if he is unbending and insists on being my enemy, then I give my word that he will pay dearly for it. My free country will give him such a tribute that he will have to complain about the shame and harm it has brought him until the end of his days."

When the giants' envoy heard this, he swiftly returned home and reported it to his king, who was furious that the king of Arimaspi actually dared to insult him like that. It was impossible to dismiss the tribute, forgive him, and let him live! His advisers then said: "Great King, you do not need to waste time on anger. We shall soon deal with him." The envoy now said: "Because he has insulted you in this manner, my advice is that you invade his country—it is a good time to do so—and engage him in battle and teach him a lesson. He would certainly already be your vassal had it not been for one wretched little man who made a really bold speech at their council, and who behaved as if all realms were subject to him! The speech he made could not have been more vigorous. Before the council had ended, he had persuaded the king not to pledge obedience to you. He is quite imposing. I have never before encountered anyone like that among the small people, and he only came up to my knee. I saw him stand before the king in his council as a worthy warrior, which surprised me then and surprises me still. Even if you do no more than take that one into your power," said the fierce envoy of the giants, "then your military operation will still have been worthwhile. Invade them right now."

The king of the giants was perturbed that this one man had spoken so forcefully against paying the tribute and swore fiercely that he would delay no longer. He would drive him away, or kill him, or capture him and have him hanged. He would have to suffer and be shamed. He called together an army of a thousand giants from his country, and with them invaded the kingdom of Arimaspi. Every one of these giants carried a long and heavy iron club as a weapon, and they made a great deal of noise as they crossed the fields and heaths. They would pay for this later.

When the people of Arimaspi heard that the giants were planning to invade their country by force, they quickly gathered together and armed themselves against the powerful army, as Duke Ernst advised them, telling them all not to be afraid. He arranged for pikes, swords, and spears to be made and said: "Now I want you all to follow me. We shall take our weapons and make our way steadily to the forest through which they will have to come, and we shall wait there. That is where we can preserve ourselves, because they will not be able to use their long iron clubs. We can take on great numbers of them, cutting and slashing so that they will regret even thinking of starting this invasion."

The giants arrived in the forest and were met by the bold and resolute warriors. As soon as they realized that they were coming under attack, the giants hit back at them with their fearsome war clubs. The duke, however, withdrew his troops into the trees, where they were safe, and hacked at the legs of the giants. The duke's strategy had clearly proved itself a good one, and the giants suffered for it. Many of them were felled by the pikes and spears, and the forest was filled with the noise of battle, and when one of the giants did fall it was like a tree that had been chopped down. The tribute that they had demanded was paid in sword-thrusts that they could not carry away with them. The giants even struck one another without damaging their enemies, and thus the giants suffered losses at the hands of their own people. Thanks to the duke, they were greatly harmed in this battle, and many were so badly wounded that they had to be carried off. Eventually three hundred powerful giants lay dead, and the rest ran away.

The battle was over. They had been unable to use their long clubs because of the trees and now fled back to the land of the Anakim. The duke did not delay for long. Once he had made sure of the victory, he asked his men to help him to take one of the giants prisoner as they were trying to get away as fast as they could. They found and surrounded one powerful giant who was unable to flee because of his severe wounds. They threatened him even more with pikes and spears and stopped him from escaping, until at last he had to abandon his iron club. The duke spared his life and handed him over to his men, who then cheerfully took him back to their home. The king of the Gigantes had failed very badly, and the king of Arimaspi was victorious. From that time on he ruled untroubled and free in his own land, and the giants never invaded again. His kingdom and reputation had been saved.

The king rejoiced in his victory and returned to his home. He sent messengers ahead to tell them that his victory over the Gigantes had been so successful. Everyone celebrated, old and young, that they had been so well defended against the huge and strong people, and they were all grateful to Duke Ernst, whose strategy had helped them to victory. When they came home, the king organized a celebration to show his great affection for the duke. The noble Ernst was afforded many honors for the fame and reputation that he had helped them to gain. They had all benefited from his great wisdom, and the worthy king gave him gold and jewels. The duke then returned happily to his own lands in Arimaspi, and everyone there, men and women, welcomed the hero, who was as dear to them all as life itself. Ernst was back.

He was very good to the giant, who was still wounded. The duke tended him with care, bandaged and treated his wounds until he became well again. Ernst made clear to him that he was very much his friend. When the giant had recovered, the duke provided good clothing for him and allowed him to go freely wherever he wished. The giant declared that he would never leave him, and he would later be of use to the great and noble duke. It is said that the giant was not more than fifteen years old, so this bold warrior had not yet reached full manhood, although there was not a pine tree in the forest that reached as far as his knee, he was so huge and fearsome.

Now the duke had in his retinue the giant and two from the Land of the Pygmies, as well as several of the long-eared people and the sciapods. The duke was meticulous in providing for them, and they got whatever they wanted and more. He kept them with him because they were so rare and strange. These curious beings would often amuse and entertain him. [5013–5332]

CHAPTER 7

THE CRUSADER

Indeed, the duke lived for a good six years in that country and governed his duchy well. One morning the noble lord chanced to be taking his ease outside his castle when he saw a ship sail into the harbor, a ship that had come from Christian Ethiopia, the land of the Moors, and he asked who owned the ship, and what news they brought. They told the duke: "We are merchants and we set out from Ethiopia but could not help being driven here by the winds. We had no intention of coming to this country. We implore you, most noble knight, for the sake of God to show us mercy and help us, lord, to preserve our lives. We shall give you as much of our goods as you would like, with no limits because we are in your hands. We would only ask that you leave enough to keep us from starvation and that we can get home alive."

When he heard this, the bold warrior realized what things were like in the country they came from. Duke Ernst asked if there was a war there, and they told him what the situation was. They said: "The troops of the king of Babylon often cause great damage to the lands of the king of Ethiopia. They have frequently attacked with very considerable force, trying to make the king renounce Christianity and so to increase the numbers of heathens and unbelievers. They regularly invade our country with a great army and have to be stopped. On many occasions they have had to give way and flee from our land because of our forces and the king's bravery in battle. He is unwavering in his belief."

When he had heard their story, the duke asked the merchants if they would help him secretly and covertly. "It has long been my desire to get to Jerusalem," he said, and if they would help him to get there, he would reward them handsomely. He was also inclined, he said, if there was a war, to stay for a time there with the king, and then move on to Jerusalem. When the merchants heard this, they were very happy indeed, and promised him faithfully that they would do whatever he said.

Late one evening the bold warrior arranged to have brought together the best things he had—gold, silver, other valuables, the finest furs and silk clothes, pearls and jewels, everything that could be used and could be taken with him, everything that he wanted—and had all this loaded onto his ship, carefully and in secret. Equally covertly he brought the giant and the other strange beings, putting every one of them on the ship that was to go to Ethiopia—sciapods, pygmies, the long-eared panotii. When all this had been accomplished, he also sought out two of the cyclops of Arimaspi, both dear to him. They came to him in secret, and he asked them to travel with him. They were happy to do so because he had been a good lord to them, and soon all of them were secretly on board. Ernst took his own men, Wetzel and the other four that I have told you about before. They were in the best of spirits as they raised up the sails and set off happily on their journey. They also had the most favorable wind ever, and so the duke and his followers got away from that land. The winds took them straight to a harbor in Ethiopia, where the duke and his men disembarked. They found lodgings where they could store all their goods, and then they were conducted to a fine castle, where the merchants met the king and told him who the duke was, and where they had encountered him, as well as how they had gotten there. Everything was explained in great detail.

The duke himself then came before the mighty king, with all his unusual companions, and the king received him with all honor: "I offer my welcome to you and to your retinue." The duke thanked him for that. His giant stood next to him, with the rest of his followers, and the king and his men were amazed to see them. They had to admit that in all honesty they had never seen anything so strange before and had never heard of such people anywhere in the whole world. They were very pleased that the duke had come to them.

The exiled duke now asked the king for permission to stay there in his service until such times as he was able to travel to Jerusalem and the Holy Land. The duke then told the king about all his adventures thus far and promised that he would serve him well if he would help him with his further travels. The mighty king replied: "Believe me, if you wish to stay with me here in my country with your giant I would keep you here forever, and would give you some of my lands so that you and your followers could live here honorably. If you wish, I shall arrange that at once."

The duke thanked him for the great honor that he had shown him but said: "There is no need for that yet, and I have not yet earned it. Once I have done you some service that seems worthwhile, then I should be able to accept with honor anything you offer me in gratitude." From then on, the good king cherished him as if he were his own son, and later on the duke would indeed come to deserve it. [5333–5504]

News reached the king that the king of Babylon was attacking his lands with a great number of warriors, leading such an extremely powerful army of heathens that no one could withstand them—they wanted to cast down and destroy all of Christendom. When the noble and worthy king was informed of this he was extremely angry and quickly set about raising an army of Christians in his country. When his princes came to the court and heard the story, every single one of them declared themselves ready to defend their land, and they swore a campaign against the heathens. They were able to assemble a great force of many thousand warriors. Then the king led his army across a broad plain. The duke was pleased that he would be able to do battle, thanked Our Lord that he could join the fighting, and declared that he would forever honor and support Him if he came back alive—those were the duke's words.

A large number of the men did not survive.

The heathen army advanced in full force, but on the day of the battle they suffered considerable losses. The very narrow approach-ways had been hacked out and made wider, and during the battle that day many amazing things happened. The duke and his men came along with the king's forces, and the giant boldly carried the standard against the heathens. The duke and his men, who were always right behind him, fought in exemplary fashion, and it would be hard for me to say how many spears he broke or how many of the enemy he cut down. His standard was borne so bravely that many lay dead around it. The battle went on all day, until the sun began to sink in the west. They hacked at armor and at limbs, and the blood flowed freely. The heathens were mostly without armor, so that the Christians wiped out many of their army, cutting and thrusting until they were able to break through their line, in which there rode the ruler of Babylon himself, who fought bravely and well.

Duke Ernst came up against him in the fighting. When he saw him, he struck the king down from his battle-charger and wounded him severely, and then the noble duke formally took him prisoner in the battle. But one of the duke's men lay dead, one of those who had traveled with him across the seas and had escaped from the griffins.

The Christians had defended their land well. The duke and his giant cut the enemy down like cattle so that the heathens had to give way, turn, and flee. They left the battlefield with many very serious wounds. The Christians were victorious everywhere on the battlefield, and the heathen army was cut to pieces to ensure the Christian victory. When they reassembled, the king was very pleased and went back to his capital city with his men. They treated the wounds of the king of the heathens, binding them up well, and when he had recovered, they sent him back to his own country, telling him to instruct his princes to support him faithfully in a treaty with the Christians, something that would help them. The heathen king offered hostages until such times as amends could be made for the harm he had caused, and said that there should be reconciliation as long as both kings lived. This was confirmed formally, and both sides now released their prisoners. They put the war behind them, so that it should never be thought of again.

Duke Ernst now broached with the king the subject of his journey to Jerusalem, since he was very concerned about the many difficulties associated with this. The king of Ethiopia was very sad that Ernst did not wish to stay, but he placed him in the hands of the king of Babylon, who was to ensure his safe passage to the city of Jerusalem. He insisted upon this, and the king of Babylon at once agreed that he would assist him wherever he wanted to go, so that he would always be thanked for this whenever the tale was told, and so that he would become even dearer to the king of Ethiopia.

Once this had all been arranged, the duke prepared for the journey. Without further delay the king of Babylon took leave of his own country and rode to the Christian king and his people. The duke also took leave of the king and his court. The noble king gave him two pack mules laden with heavy gold, and also a fine dromedary, and the exiled duke and his whole company now rode off together with the king of Babylon toward Alexandria. The warrior stayed at the court of the heathen king for a month or more, and then he reminded the king of his solemn duty to bring him to Jerusalem, as he had promised. At once the king sent for four of his men who would conduct the duke to Jerusalem, and on account of his bravery gave the warrior so much gold and rich clothing that a camel could barely carry it all. The king gave him many other great honors.

    Then the noble duke took his leave and was very happy to set off with two thousand men toward Jerusalem. When he came close to Jerusalem, and the people there got word that the duke, of whom so many amazing stories had been told, was on his way, they were all delighted. They went out on foot and on horseback to meet him a mile away so that they could welcome the great hero into their country with all due honor. Then they conducted the noble lord at once to the Church of the Holy Sepulchre, where the warrior made an offering to the glory of God at the holy tomb. He dedicated half of his unusual creatures to the Church, together with much of his riches that he had brought with him—jewels, gold, and fine material. He made an equally great offering at the Temple, and to all the other holy places. The worthy warrior stayed for more than a year in the Holy Land, and while he was there, often fought fiercely against the heathens. The great hero was often seen riding out, instilling fear and doing battle with the heathens whenever he encountered them, so that the heathens were hurt and shamed, while his warriors came through it all with honor. He was a man of considerable worth and esteem. In the year Duke Ernst spent there he was never idle and constantly harassed the heathens; he was always fighting them, and they hated him. [5505–5704]

CHAPTER 8

THE PENITENT RESTORED

At this time a group of pilgrims from Germany came there from across the sea and gave the duke a full and honest account of how he was regarded at home. Many of them took back news of him when they returned home. In this way the emperor learned that he was in Jerusalem and was in good health, the news brought to him by a knight who had seen him there. He gave the emperor a full and detailed account of Ernst's strange retinue and of all the adventures he had had, and how he himself had seen and was in a position to report on the amazing creatures and say honestly that they were still with him. The great emperor was pleased to pass on to all of his princes the news that Duke Ernst was alive and well in Jerusalem.

When this became known to the princes, they worried about his life. They said, "He should now be forgiven for what he did, and we must help the noble lord regain the imperial favor, so that his guilt can be wiped out and he can return to the good graces of the emperor."

By the grace of God and with the intercession of Empress Adelaide, the emperor himself came to regret that he had done Duke Ernst an injustice because Count Henry had slandered him. The mighty emperor ordered, therefore, that he should return in secret to the empire. He wished to restore to him everything that he had taken away, and wanted to forgive the brave warrior everything and bestow great gifts on him. That was what he had in mind. [5705–5756]

To continue with the story, then.

As long as the noble duke was in Jerusalem, the worthy warrior was cherished for his great bravery. He did so much harm to the heathens that they had good cause to bewail their losses. The duke now heard regularly that the great Holy Roman emperor had spoken mercifully of him and had often prayed to the Lord that he might return to his homeland, so that he might hear of all the marvels that had happened. Every one of the imperial princes spoke well of him, too. Therefore, the young duke took leave of Jerusalem and all its people and asked the way from the city to the port of Acre, where he took ship.

They were on the sea for over six weeks, and the winds were such that they suffered a great deal. His remaining sciapod died, and this affected the duke greatly. Then the ship reached the port of Bari, where he was very well received.

Before they left Bari, the bold warrior made a thank-offering at the tomb of Saint Nicholas of Myra there, willingly giving them fine cloth and strips of gold. Then he left and soon reached Rome, where the people, when they heard of his arrival, received him with great honor. Many men came on foot and on horseback and accompanied him to the great basilica of Saint Peter, rich in holy relics. Here, too, he made an offering of silk and of cloth of gold, the best that could be found. Before he traveled farther, the bold man was entertained with great honor in Rome. They kept the noble duke there for more than a week and would not let him go before they had heard about every one of his experiences. His collection of curious beings amazed them.

Then the noble duke commended them to the care of the Lord, since he wanted to take his leave. They were sorry about this but had to let him go, also with God's blessing, and so the warrior came from there back to Bavaria, although he did so without anyone knowing. He sent a message in secret to one of his trusted vassals that he should remain there incognito. His liegeman then told him that a meeting of the court was to be held at Bamberg, where the emperor was to appear in state. In fact, it would be for Mass on Christmas Day—that had been planned.

"You, my lord, and Earl Wetzel should both come in secret. I shall conceal your companions, if you will let me, so that you can attend without fear, because you will not be recognized while you are there." They thought this was a good idea and set off for Bamberg. Late on Christmas Eve the bold warriors waited in a forest nearby until it was almost time for early Mass and then covertly entered the city, where they went in secret to the empress and found her at her prayers. They prostrated themselves before the empress, and when she saw them, she asked who they were. The earl told her that it was the duke, her son, and asked that she should show him grace and help him back into favor, so that the emperor might by the grace of God forgive him. The empress jumped up and embraced her son, kissing him often, with tears in her eyes. She told the duke to go in secret to her lodgings and told him not to appear in front of the emperor before he had heard the Nativity Mass sung, and only then to present himself to him. He should arrange to fall at his feet when the Gospel was being read. "In the meantime I shall speak with the princes and enlist their help."

With that, the duke went back into hiding. He could see that this day would bring an end to all his problems, and by God's grace this was indeed the case. After her conversation, the empress at once called together the princes and told them confidentially about the return of her son, and that he was hoping that they would favor him and for the sake of God plead with the emperor on his behalf, so that he might—with their support—agree to show him grace and pardon him. The empress promised to use all the influence that she might have on behalf of the worthy warrior. The emperor would have to restore him to his favor, or at least pardon him. The princes all promised their support, which pleased the empress. [5757–5907]

The emperor put on his royal regalia, and the princes all came into the cathedral. The emperor, wearing the imperial crown, stood beside the empress, as was usual on ceremonial occasions. A bishop sang Mass before them, and there was a great throng of people in the huge cathedral. When the Gospel was to be read, the bishop went to the lectern and declaimed the word of Our Beloved Lord to the Christian people. Ernst and Wetzel did not wait any longer but came forward, barefoot and in the woolen garments of penitents, threw themselves at the emperor's feet, and begged him for his mercy. The princes all came forward, too, and one after another urged him for the sake of Almighty God and the sacrifice of Christ that he should, in honor of the most holy day, grant grace to this man.

"For whatever he did, even had he taken my life, let him be forgiven by the grace of God. I will set all things aside."

He had not yet recognized the duke. He raised him up and embraced him, and Ernst thanked him in proper fashion. Then the great ruler looked him in the eyes and recognized him, and now regretted what had happened. When he became aware of who he was, the emperor moved aside and did not want to speak to him. But the princes all said: "Great and mighty emperor, you should allow to stand what you said so publicly in the face of the whole empire. You forgave him for our sake and in the name of God, and it would be a disgrace if you now acted against it."

"Very well, if you, the princes, want him to be pardoned, then I shall turn away from my anger, and he shall evermore be dear to me." He gave him gifts of silver and gold and recompensed him generously. The princes all dismissed any claims they might have had upon him, and rejoiced in the fact that he had come home.

When the sung Mass had come to an end, the nobles all thronged around them, received them with honor, and made them welcome. Ernst's mother, the empress, was extremely happy to see her son. The emperor then asked him where his wonderful retinue was, and the noble duke replied, "In Bavaria," and the emperor sent fast messengers who traveled day and night and eventually brought them all to the imperial court. Everyone who saw them found them very strange indeed, and all said that this was a once-in-a-lifetime sight. Then the emperor asked Ernst to give him some of the amazing creatures. Ernst was reluctant to do so, and at first refused, but then he gave him one of the cyclops, one of the long-eared people (who sang especially well), and one of the pygmies. The rest he retained for himself, taking the giant back to his home in Bavaria, not wishing anyone else to have charge of him. The emperor kept the duke for twelve days with him at court, so that he could tell him everything about where he had gotten these many wonderful creatures, allowing him to leave nothing out; he presided over no judicial cases and did not even leave his room until he had heard the whole amazing tale.

Furthermore, the emperor gave orders for it to be written down why and how he had exiled the duke, how long he had remained at home, how he had left, and how he had returned. All who heard the duke's story were deeply moved. Then the emperor restored to the noble lord all his lands, and the duke ruled thereafter with great honor in the lands he had inherited. He cared for his lands and his people in exemplary fashion, giving gifts and distributing fiefs as a ruler should.

The emperor was not satisfied until Ernst was as rich and powerful as he had been before, and he cherished him until the day he died.

And so Duke Ernst had overcome all adversity. [5908–6022]

KONRAD VON WÜRZBURG

HENRY OF KEMPTEN

There was once an emperor named Otto, to whom a great many countries were subject, all of them held in thrall by fear of his power. He had a fine long beard, which he tended with considerable care, and anything that he swore "by my beard" would be carried out to the letter. He had fiery red hair and was, all things considered, an unpleasant man, who proved time and again how anger and rage could just boil up inside him. Anyone who tried to go against him was as good as dead, and if the emperor said of anyone, "You'll pay for that, by my beard," then that person would be killed on the spot without any hope of mercy. A lot of men had lost their lives that way after falling out of favor with the emperor over some serious misdemeanor.

One year, Otto decided to hold a great Easter celebration at his fine and large fortress near Bamberg, and a great number of high-ranking prince-abbots from royal monasteries came to this feast, as well as many worthy bishops. A whole stream of earls, barons, and knights with their richly dressed retinues came, too, all of whom owed feudal allegiance to the empire and to its imperial leader. The dignitaries all thronged to this imperial diet peacefully and happily. Once the paschal Mass had been celebrated, everything was going well, tables were set up and looked splendid, bread was put out ready, and there were plenty of fine goblets, too, so that when Emperor Otto and his court came back from the cathedral, they could wash their hands and break their fast straightaway. [1–49]

A young and noble squire had been sent to the festival to learn proper courtly behavior, a wellborn, good-looking, and clearly good-hearted lad, who was much admired by everyone there. His father was the powerful duke of Swabia, and one day he would inherit all his great wealth as the sole heir. This same innocent lad was at court that day and wandered along the tables. The noble youngster put out his immaculately clean hand and took a piece of white bread, then broke off a tiny piece to eat, the sort of thing youngsters do without thinking, simply wanting to sneak an early mouthful.

Just as this noble squire was taking the bread and breaking off a small piece, the emperor's high steward happened to be passing, his staff in his hand, supervising what the guests were going to eat when they came back from hearing Mass. When he saw that the youngster had fancied a taste of the bread, he at once flew into a rage, because he was the sort of person who could be set off by the smallest thing. He ran across to the nobly born and good-looking youngster and hit him so hard with the staff he was carrying that red blood soaked the boy's head and his hair, and he fell to the ground and sat there crying bitterly. That the steward had dared to strike the boy was witnessed by a warrior, an especially bold knight called Henry of Kempten. This knight was an upstanding and brave nobleman with a strong sense of honor, and he had (I understand) come with the young squire from Swabia as his guardian, a task he carried out very conscientiously. He was most upset and extremely angry that this wellborn lad should have been given such a beating. The resolute warrior went up to the steward and demanded furiously: "What do you think you are doing, breaking every rule of courtly decency, and striking the son of a powerful duke so viciously! Let me tell you that this kind of insulting behavior, knocking down my master's son for no reason at all, is simply intolerable."

"It's none of your business," replied the steward. "I'm perfectly entitled to teach ill-bred brats a lesson and punish anyone who offends against courtly etiquette here, so you should just keep quiet. I'm about as afraid of you as a hawk would be of a hen! And anyway, if I have insulted the duke by giving his son a beating, what do you propose to do about it!"

"You'll soon see," replied Henry of Kempten, "and you'll be sorry here and now for hitting the duke's heir. I am not going to stand for this, you miserable wretch, you don't deserve to live after giving the child such a beating! And because you committed such a disgraceful act with your grubby hands, your own blood has to spill on the ground right here in this hall!" Henry picked up a great cudgel, a massive club, and brought it down on the steward's skull, smashing it like an egg and splitting it in two as if it were a clay pot, so that the man spun around, his brains (I should imagine) beaten from his head. He collapsed onto the ground and lay there quite dead. The hall was red with his blood, and there was a loud outcry and a huge commotion. [50–158]

By now the emperor had also returned, had ceremonially washed his hands, and had taken his seat at the table. He saw the blood spilled on the floor and said: "What happened here? Who has defiled this hall and done so much damage that there is blood everywhere?" His inner circle of courtiers quickly told him that his steward had just been killed. "And who has caused me distress by doing that?"

"It was Henry of Kempten," they all replied. "Indeed," said the mighty emperor, "if he did kill him, then he should have stayed where he was in Swabia. Have him sent to me at once, so that I can find out why he has inflicted this great loss upon me."

The knight was duly summoned to come before the fearsome emperor, and as soon as Otto laid eyes upon him, he flew into a rage and said: "Sir, how could you behave in such an outrageous way as to murder my high steward? You have incurred my greatest displeasure, and you will soon feel the force of my imperial power for having insulted this court and my own position. We shall take vengeance for this dreadful deed, that you were seen to kill my own steward."

"No, Majesty," said Henry resolutely. "I ask for mercy and for your good grace. Give me a hearing and then judge if I am guilty or innocent. If I have by my impetuous behavior earned your disfavor, then may your majesty strike me down and blacken my name. But if I can show that I was *not* the guilty party, then I ask for your mercy and that you do not punish me. In the name of our Savior, who rose again on this Easter Day, grant me the chance to regain your imperial grace. Your wisdom is part of your very being, so do honor to this assembly in the sight of all those worthies gathered here today and let this poor wretch live. There is no sin so great that it cannot be forgiven, so I am begging you for the grace that I may be allowed to live."

The bad-tempered redheaded emperor gave him a grim answer: "The pains of death inflicted upon my steward cause me so much personal hurt that I am not at all inclined to show you any mercy, and through your most vicious behavior you have forfeited forever my imperial grace. By my beard, you shall pay for the fact that my steward is lying there dead, struck down by your hand and without any reason." [159–244]

When the noble Henry heard the oath uttered by the fearsome emperor, he realized that he would lose his life there on the spot. This made him so angry that he resolved to defend himself and make every effort to save his life, because he knew very well that whatever the emperor swore by his beard would be carried out in full. He said to himself, "Well, it looks as if I am condemned to death, so it is time to defend myself and fight for my life as hard as I can." And with that, the fine warrior leaped very quickly indeed at the emperor, grabbed him by the beard, and dragged him half across the table. All the fine dishes, fish or flesh, that had been placed before the emperor went flying when Henry grabbed him by the beard, tearing out a lot of hair as he did so. Otto's imperial head suffered great indignity, as the state crown and other imperial regalia that the emperor was wearing fell onto the floor of the palace. Henry had by now very quickly taken hold of him and taken from his belt a sharp dagger, which he held at Otto's throat, squeezing his neck with the other hand. He said: "Now you are to give me protection and an assurance that you are granting me your grace and mercy, because if you do not, then you will lie dead on the ground. If you want to live, then take back that oath that you swore, or these will be your last moments!"

Henry sprawled on top of him, gripping the emperor's long beard hard and throttling him so much that he could barely speak.

The other high-ranking and brave lords all jumped up and ran toward them, as the emperor, deathly pale, lay there in the hands of Henry of Kempten. The perilous position of the emperor drove them to try to rescue him, but Henry said: "If anyone touches me, then the emperor dies, and I shall take down the first man who attacks me. If I am to die, then so does our noble host. This sharp dagger will put an end to his right to rule. His guests will be treated just like our host if you try to kill me. I can spill a lot of blood before I'm brought down. Come on, then! If one of you wants to die, come and attack me!" With that they all backed away, as indeed they had to. The emperor struggled to signal to them that they should move away. [245–328]

As soon as they had done so, Henry, still undaunted, said to the emperor: "If you want to live, then don't make me stay like this any longer. Give me a guarantee that I am not to be killed and I shall spare your life. If you do not give me safe conduct, then you are a dead man." At that the emperor raised his hand for a formal oath and swore on his imperial honor that Henry could leave at once without harm.

When this promise of safe conduct had been given, Henry at once allowed Emperor Otto to get up. He also let go of his beard. As soon as he was on his feet, the emperor went and took his seat again on his richly decorated throne. He smoothed his hair and beard and addressed Henry of Kempten again. "I have granted you safe conduct and guaranteed your life. But you are to ensure that in the future our paths should never cross and that I never set eyes upon you again. It has become very clear to me that you are too much of a problem to be part of my court. Furthermore, you have insulted me very thoroughly indeed, and anyone would need simply to glance at my beard to see that I shall be more than happy to avoid your company forever. In future I shall find a different barber to trim my beard, you can be sure of that. As God is my witness, my beard will be kept well away from your razor, since your efforts can cause a lot of damage to royal skin and hair. I have learned by bitter experience that you are a terrible barber. You must leave my court and lands before sunset today." At that, Henry took leave of the imperial court at once and made off as quickly as he could.

* * *

The records say that Henry returned to Swabia and settled down in his own well-appointed estates near Kempten, where he had fields, both grazing and arable land, which he held as a feudal warrior bound to the royal abbey of Kempten. A reliable source indicates that he lived there blamelessly. He was well off and was held in some esteem. [329–393]

* * *

A good ten years or more later, it so happened that Emperor Otto was involved in a major military campaign and was besieging a fine and important city beyond the Alps. He and his forces had spent a long time trying to bring down this fortress with his stone-hurling siege machines and his archers, but he had reached the point at which he needed more troops, and he sent word that German knights were to be recruited. He sent out word to the most important noblemen everywhere that anyone who had feudal obligations to the empire should come to his aid immediately and without any delay. At the same time, he reminded the princes and dukes that everyone who was under imperial obligation because they held their estates as fiefs from the crown should come at once to Puglia to provide military support. If anyone of them failed to do so, he would forfeit his tenure and would have to leave his lands. When this message was sent to all parts of the German empire, the news also came to the abbot at Kempten.

When the noble prince-abbot received the imperial command, he prepared to set off to war, and himself sent word very quickly, it seems, to his feudal knights, who were commanded on the strength of their oaths of allegiance and loyalty to go with him. The prince-abbot also summoned the seasoned warrior Henry of Kempten and said: "You will certainly have heard that the emperor has sent word to his German lands to recruit forces. As one of his princes I am obliged to cross the Alps to assist him, and I badly need you and your men with me. I am calling all my men out, with you at their head, to come with me and join in the campaign. I am pledged to do so, and so are you. Go, then, and prepare for us to go to war."

"My lord," said Henry of Kempten, "What are you saying! You must know that I dare not appear before the emperor and his court, because I forfeited any chance of his favor. Please release me from the obligation of taking part in this campaign in view of my service to you. The emperor withdrew his favor from me completely and very clearly and put me under pain of death. I have two grown-up sons, my lord, and I can send them with you—take these two, well armed and ready to fight, rather than myself."

"No," replied the prince-abbot, "I have no intention of taking those two in your place, as you ask, because you are of such great value to me. At a time like this my esteem and feelings of confidence all depend upon you. You are a superb strategist in military matters, and you are the best man to deal with anything important that happens at the imperial court, far better than anyone else. Therefore, there is not a single man who would be more useful to me on this campaign than you, and that is why I am asking you to give me your support and your ever-reliable counsel. If, however, you continue to object and refuse me your service, then by God I shall take away the estates you hold as fiefs from me and give them to someone who understands that they must be earned."

"If you really mean that you would give my estates to someone else if I don't obey you," said the knight, "then, God knows, I shall have to ride with you, whatever fears I might have about joining this particular campaign right now. I would rather ride with you—even if it leads to my death—than surrender my estates and my position. I am duty-bound to come to provide you with my support when needed because you are my feudal lord, and I owe you my service. Since you are determined not to release me from this obligation, your command shall be obeyed. I shall willingly suffer whatever ills the emperor might decide to inflict upon me so that I can fulfill my proper service to you on this campaign." [394–511]

And so the brave vassal set out on the campaign and traveled with his overlord across the Alps. He was so bold and resolute that he never gave way to his fears. He did what his lord commanded and behaved just as a feudal warrior should. They soon reached the city that was being so fiercely besieged by the Holy Roman emperor and his army. Henry of Kempten took care to keep out of the emperor's sight and never appear in his presence, afraid to do so because of the old enmity between them, and his own guilt. Because of this, Henry, that most valiant warrior, kept out of his way, and set up his camp a small distance away from the others.

One day (so I have read) he had a bath prepared, because he needed to refresh himself after the long journey, a bath he took in a wooden tub that had been requisitioned from a nearby village. Well concealed, the knight was sitting in this tub when he saw a group of citizens from the besieged town come down, and the great emperor came riding forward and approached them, wanting to parley about the fate of the city. These treacherous citizens had, however, prepared a devious trap and were intending to kill him; having engaged him in debate, they were planning to assassinate him in an act of straightforward murder. I think that what happened was this: the moment the emperor rode forward, completely unarmed, a hidden ambush had been set for him, and as he rode toward them unaware, he found himself under attack by treacherous hands. The murderous mob who had secretly planned his downfall now rushed at him with naked swords drawn and ready, intending to cause him harm.

When Sir Henry of Kempten—who was still there in his tub—saw this wicked homicidal attack, this treacherous attempt on the life of Emperor Otto, he abandoned his bath and, proving himself a true hero, leaped out of the deep tub and ran to where his shield was hanging on a wall, grabbing it and seizing hold as he did so of a fine sword, and with these arms the naked warrior sprinted toward the emperor. He managed to free him from the attackers who had come from the city and—still naked—defended him. A good few of the enemy were hacked and cut down, and he killed those who were trying to murder the emperor, spilling their blood with all his strength as he harried them to a bitter death with great blows, until any that were left alive simply fled. As soon as the valiant knight had rescued the emperor, he immediately rushed back, naked as he was, and got back into his bathtub, continuing his bath and behaving as if he had no idea what had been happening. [512–603]

The emperor meanwhile had fled back to his own men. He had no idea of who it was that had so bravely rescued him, because he had not recognized him. He rode back to his tent, dismounted, and sat down on his throne in an angry mood. All his highest-ranking noblemen quickly thronged around him, and he said: "My lords, you realize that I was very nearly betrayed! Had it not been for the capable hands of the knight who came to my aid, it would have been all over for me, and I would have been killed. If I only knew who had done me such a valiant service—fighting naked to save me—I would reward him with lands and riches, since I owe my very life to his brave assistance. Surely there can never have been a bolder warrior, nor a braver one. If any of you knows who it was, then in God's name bring him here to stand before me. I declare here and now that he shall be richly rewarded. He has my heart, and he shall forever be in my favor. Nowhere in the world will you ever find a more worthy knight!"

There were some in the group standing there who knew perfectly well that it had been Henry of Kempten who had been on the spot to save the emperor, and several of them came forward to say: "Majesty, we know exactly who the hero was who saved your illustrious life from being cut off by death, only as things are at the moment, the burden of your displeasure rests very heavily upon his shoulders. He is unfortunate enough to have caused you—and it was his own fault—to withdraw your favor from him. If there is a chance that grace can be granted to him again, then we shall bring him here before you." "Even if he had killed my own father," the emperor assured them, "I would restore him to my favor and show him grace. I swear this on my own faith and on my imperial honor."

With that, they told him that it was Henry of Kempten, and the mighty emperor spoke again without hesitation: "If he came here on this campaign, then I am very glad of it. Who else would have dared to fight naked, as he did today? After all, he was the one who also had the effrontery to drag an emperor across the table by his beard. His nature is clearly bold and resolute, and he is certainly not going to be punished for that. No, from now on he can count on my support and protection. I think, however, I shall give him a bit of a fright first and receive him as if I were severe and angry." Accordingly, he gave orders for Henry to be brought to the court as soon as possible, and he was taken before him in a very hostile manner, and yes, the emperor received him with a show of great hatred. [604–685]

"Explain to me," said the great emperor, "how you could have dared to come here and how you could ever let me set eyes on you again? You must know only too well why and how I became your sworn enemy. Surely you were the one who decided to trim my beard without using a razor, and it was your wild and furious behavior that robbed it of so much hair that to this day it has lost its curl? Yes, it *was* you who perpetrated that outrage. The fact that you have dared come to this country makes it abundantly clear that you are still just as arrogant and full of yourself!"

"Mercy, Majesty," said the warrior, "I was compelled to come here by my obligations, and because of that I beg and implore you to forgive me for what I did. My overlord the prince-abbot, who is here today, commanded me in the name of the obedience due to him that I could under no circumstances refuse to come with him on this campaign. I swear here—as I may be saved—that I set out against my will, and did so, as God is my witness, so that I could fulfill my obligations. Had I not come with him and set out on the campaign he would have taken my estates away from me."

The emperor burst out laughing. "You are an excellent warrior," he said, "and it is clear to me that you are quite blameless, so because of that, I am happy to put my quarrel with you aside and bid you a thousand times welcome in God's name! You came to my rescue when I was in great trouble and saved my life. I should, most blessed sir, have died, had it not been for you." With that he jumped up and ran over to Henry and kissed his face and his hands, so that a full reconciliation and peace was established between them once again. All hostility between them was now at an end, as the noble emperor's bitter anger was no longer directed at the knight. He rewarded Henry with gifts of money, and with a grant of land that carried with it an income of two hundred silver marks, so the knight's indomitable bravery had earned him great riches and also fame and honor among men, and for this he is remembered to this day.

All this shows that every knight should show boldness and avoid holding back in a cowardly fashion. Sadly, bravery and chivalric behavior are both very rare these days. For all that, they will still bring fame and honor to any man able to display them and to live by them as precepts.

*   *   *

Thus ends the tale of Henry of Kempten. I wrote it (translating it into German from Latin) at the request of my lord of Tiersberg, and I did so in the fine city of Strasbourg, where he is provost of the cathedral, and where he enjoys great esteem as the shining flower of all the clergy. Since he has so many splendid virtues, God will increase His blessings upon him, and I, Konrad von Würzburg, shall always pray for him, because he has never failed to increase, by his great generosity, the honor in which he is held.

The story ends here. [686–770]

HEINRICH

*REYNARD
THE FOX*

This is the tale of Reynard the Fox.

May God guide us on our journey!

What I am about to tell you is an unusual, but entirely believable story about a wild animal, and it may serve as an instructive fable in a great many ways. The animal in question was entirely focused upon deceit and trickery, which often led him into trouble. He indulged in all kinds of wickedness, and his name was Reynard the Fox. So let us begin the story.

CHAPTER 1

THE FOX AND THE COCKEREL

A very well-off farmer was living comfortably in a field by a village. He had money and property, and plenty of corn and millet, and the land was well plowed. His name was Lanzelin, and his wife was known as Gammer Runzela. He did have one problem, and that was the fact that he was forever trying to protect his chickens from Reynard the Fox. His farmyard did not have a proper fence, and he suffered a number of losses, about which he was very unhappy. So Gammer Runzela said to her husband: "Lanzelin, you're an old fool! I've already lost ten of my hens to Reynard, and that makes me really cross and angry." Farmer Lanzelin had been given a scolding, and he couldn't do anything about it, so he did what Gammer Runzela had told him to do and put up a solid fence, behind which he thought that Chantecler the cockerel—whom Reynard had long wanted to take—and his wives would be well protected.

One day, however, just as the sun was rising, Reynard thought that he could not resist it, and went off to the farmyard with malicious intent—he had a wicked plan in mind about Chantecler. He realized that the fence was too high and thick, so he broke off a splinter of it with his teeth and made sure he was not observed. He was happy to see that there was no one about, so he wriggled through a hedge and managed to lie down quite close to Chantecler. Reynard was the archenemy of Chantecler, who was asleep right by the wall. Pinte the hen spotted Reynard and shouted out, "My lord!" and flew up onto a perch, followed by the other wives. Chantecler hurried over to them and told them to go back to the wall where they had been. "You don't have to worry about any animals here in this fenced enclosure, although you should pray to God, my dear ladies, that He might protect me. Truth to tell, I had an extremely unpleasant dream. I dreamt that I was wearing a red fur coat, with bones around the collar, and I'm afraid that that spells trouble. May prayers be sent up to my guardian angel that I come out of it well, because I am very depressed about it." His wife, Pinte, said: "My beloved lord, I saw something moving in the bushes. If my feelings are not deceiving me, there is something wicked afoot, though I don't know what it is. May Almighty God preserve you! I have a really bad feeling, I'm worried and afraid that we might run into trouble, I'm telling you." Chantecler replied: "On my life, a woman is more fearful than four men put together. We've been told over and over again that dreams only come true after seven years." Madam Pinte said: "Don't be angry, but just fly up onto that thornbush. Don't forget that our children are still very small. If you were to lose your life, I should become a pitiful widow woman, left destitute forever. It troubles my heart that I am so fearful for you. May our good Lord protect and keep you!"

Chantecler flew up onto the thorn-branch, from which Reynard was eventually able to grab him. Pinte made off very quickly, and Reynard appeared underneath the branch, but Chantecler was too high up for him. The fox had to draw on his great reserves of cunning, and asked: "Who is that up there? It that you, Sengelin?" "No," replied Chantecler, "I'm not him— that was my father's name." "I see," said Reynard, "and I mourn the death of your late father. He was always gracious even to the meanest of folk. Family connections are a great thing, but I must say that you yourself behave a little distantly. Your father got on well with my father, and never sat so high up. Whatever time of day he saw my father he would never fail to fly down to welcome him. He would flap his wings, shut both his eyes, and sing to him, good-natured fowl that he was."

Chantecler said: "Then that is what I shall do! My father brought me up properly, so I welcome you with great pleasure!" He flapped his wings and jumped down happily. The fool was in too much of a hurry, and he soon came to regret it. The moment he shut his eyes and started to sing, Reynard took him by the throat. Pinte screamed and began to wail, but without further ado, Reynard trotted off toward the woods.

Farmer Lanzelin heard the noise and cried, "Oh God, it's my chickens!" and Chantecler said to Reynard: "Why are you in such a hurry? Why are you letting that farmer shout at you? Can't you give as good as you get?" "You're right, dammit," said Reynard, and shouted back, "You're wasting your time!" When he did so, Chantecler, who had been far from happy where he was, was more than delighted to pull his neck away from Reynard's mouth and saved himself by flying up into a tree. Reynard was not best pleased by this, and Chantecler, looking down at Reynard, said: "You were doing me a favor I didn't ask for, and the trip here seemed a bit long to me. Come what may, I can tell you that you won't be taking me back." Reynard could hardly miss the mocking tone, and said: "By God, you would have to be really stupid to try and take revenge when being chased and likely to be put in danger. And you also have to be stupid to make a noise when you would do better to keep your mouth shut." To this Chantecler said, "God knows, you'd be brighter still if you always thought about what you were doing." That was the end of their recriminations, because Farmer Lanzelin was coming, and Reynard had to get away quickly. He was furious that he had lost the meal he was hoping to have, and he started to feel very hungry indeed. [1–176]

CHAPTER 2

THE FOX AND THE BLUETIT

At this point Reynard heard a little bluetit and said: "Greetings, my dear friend! I am really in the mood to kiss you, but God knows you are being very standoffish. My dear friend, you should demonstrate your love and trust—God Himself would be sorry if I were to find you wanting in that respect! In the name of all that I owe to your child, whose godfather I am, I am your faithful and open friend." The bluetit replied: "I've heard quite a lot of bad things about you, Reynard, and I'm afraid of your eyes, which look very cruel to me. If you keep them shut, then I'll be happy to kiss you three times on the mouth." Reynard was very pleased at this tasty little prospect and was greatly looking forward to it. His dear friend, however, was still sitting high up in a tree. Reynard screwed his eyes shut, just as his friend had instructed. The bluetit picked up a piece of dirt in her foot, hopped from one branch another and dropped it neatly into Reynard's mouth. Now she saw clearly her friend's wicked plan. With bared teeth he grabbed at the piece of dirt, but his bluetit friend got out of his way. He had put in a lot of effort for a very poor reward and was again most unhappy about it. "Oh Lord," he said, "how could You let a little bird trick me like that! I am really, really cross about it!" [177–216]

CHAPTER 3

THE FOX AND THE CROW

Reynard was a master of trickery, but today was not a day on which things were going to work out well for him. He now spotted, high above him, a crow called Dizelin, who had cunningly managed to get hold of some fresh cheese, and wicked Reynard was disinclined to let the crow eat it on his own. Accordingly, he applied his mind fully to how he could trick him out of it with a cunning lie. Reynard sat down under the tree in which the crow was about to gobble up the cheese and said: "Is that you, Dizelin! Your old pal is really pleased to find himself in your company—there is nothing in the world that could give me greater pleasure! What I would like most is for you to sing, so I can hear if you are as good as your father, who could really belt it out!"

"Nothing against my father," replied Dizelin, "but I am happy to say, and can do so without fear of contradiction, that not one of my forebears could sing better than I can." With that he began to sing, and the entire forest shook with the noise. Reynard begged him to sing one of his own tunes for him. When he started to sing up in the branches, the bird forgot about the cheese. Reynard, however, had no intention of eating it up immediately, even though it had fallen right by his mouth. Let me tell you how the false trickster Reynard plotted the death of the bird, even though he had no need to do so.

"Listen, Dizelin," he said, "you have to help me, dear friend. You don't know that unfortunately I have a serious problem. Earlier today I hurt myself. That cheese is right next to me, and it smells really strongly, and I'm worried that it might affect the wound I got. My dear friend, help me out. Your father was always very loyal, and they say that you can't water down a good bloodline. You friend could well die, but you could easily do something about it. The stench is really making me suffer."

The crow immediately flew down, and Reynard deceived him. The crow wanted to help him in his suffering, and it nearly cost him his life. Reynard began to cough, and the crow went to take the cheese away, thinking that he was helping. Reynard leaped up—looking surprisingly free of any wounds—and showed his friend just how trustworthy he was, though he didn't even know himself what he was taking revenge for. He tore out a lot of feathers, and the crow only just managed to escape. Reynard was too much of a trickster for him. [217–284]

CHAPTER 4

THE FOX AND THE DOGS

Reynard now had to run away, because a hunter and his dogs were on his trail, and this situation did not please him. The hunter set four dogs after the fox, and they soon found him. He even had to abandon the cheese, so his friend Dizelin could claim his right to it after all. The dogs were nearly on him, and Dizelin did what he could to cause him problems, shouting at him in fury, "They tell me that dirty deeds can be paid back in full, and that's what has happened to you—friend!" Reynard twisted away from the dogs, but the crow didn't lose interest in the matter but pointed the dogs toward Reynard's tail. This was not the best thing that could happen to him, and the dogs tore at him while the hunter egged them on. It was time for some clever trickery; Reynard spotted a fallen tree trunk and slipped under it, the dogs all jumped over it, with the hunter after them, and Reynard escaped into the forest. [285–312]

CHAPTER 5

THE FOX AND THE TOMCAT

In the forest he met Tibert, the tomcat. Reynard embraced him and claimed: "A thousand welcomes, my friend! I am absolutely delighted to find you looking so well. I've heard a great deal about how fast you can run, and that is something I should like to see. If it's true, I'll tell everyone about it."

Tibert replied, "Reynard my friend, I'm pleased that such good things are being said about me, and I shall be happy to oblige you." Reynard, however, was not being honest. He sent the cat off in a direction where he knew there was a gin trap—this was a wicked act from a so-called friend. It was a narrow track he had to run down. "Now let me see how strong you are, off you go, my dear fellow!" said Reynard. Tibert, however, knew all about the trap and said to himself, "May Saint Gallus preserve me from Reynard's dirty deeds!" He jumped over the trap and ran hard. When he reached the turnaround marker, Reynard said to him: "There isn't an animal faster than you, my dear friend, but let me teach you an extra trick. You have to be able to jump really high, because otherwise it could be the end of you if you were being chased by a savage dog—and I know what I am talking about there!"

"You don't need to tell me," replied Tibert. "Just run after me and I'll demonstrate the finest jumps possible." Each of them was intending to deceive the other. Reynard ran after his friend, who did not keep very far in front. Tibert leaped over the trap, then stopped stock-still, which made his companion cannon into him so that—as he so richly deserved—his foot went into the trap. With this, Tibert took his leave, commenting before he made a rapid escape that the devil takes the hindmost.

Reynard was in very considerable trouble and thought that he would meet a grim death. At this point he saw the hunter who had set the trap. Reynard needed now more than ever to use his cunning. He laid his head over the trap just as the hunter, a farmer, ran up to it. Reynard's throat was as white as snow, and the hunter felt certain of getting a bounty of five silver pieces, maybe even more. He swung the axe back and brought it down as hard as he could. Reynard could not get away, but he pulled his head aside just at the right moment. The farmer struck the trap itself and smashed it. Reynard had never been luckier—he had thought that he would lose his life and that his white fur would be sold for five pieces of silver. Now he did not hesitate, and as quickly as possible left behind him a place that had been far from comfortable. The dejected farmer watched him go, cursing himself now that he would have to find some other source of cash. [313–384]

CHAPTER 6

THE FOX AND THE WOLF

Soon after Reynard had escaped from this dangerous situation, he met the wolf, Isengrim, and as soon as he saw him, this is what he said: "God give you good day, my lord! Whatever service I may offer to you and to milady your wife, just ask and you may be sure I shall do it. In fact, I came here to warn you because I have heard that you are widely hated. Will you accept me as a companion? I am clever, you are strong, and you would find me very useful. With your strength and my cunning we should be unbeatable. I could conquer us a castle!"

Isengrim consulted his wife and two sons on the matter, and they all agreed that the wolf should take him in as part of the family, something that he later came to regret quite considerably. Reynard was head-over-heels in love with Hirsent, Isengrim's wife, and she was the one he really wanted to serve. Isengrim had acquired, therefore, an evil companion who would cause a great amount of damage. [385–412]

CHAPTER 7

THE FOX AND THE SHE-WOLF

One day it so happened that Isengrim took his two sons, and they set off into the country to look for plunder. He took his wife by the hand and impressed upon her that Reynard was loyal and honorable. Reynard, however, wanted to woo his kinswoman, and Lord Isengrim had indeed taken on a wicked chamberlain.

The story gets very interesting at this point.

Reynard said to the lady: "My kinswoman, would that you could see the great sorrow that I have. The great love I feel for you is a pain that is hard to bear."

"Be quiet, Reynard," replied Isengrim's wife. "My lord is strong and handsome, and I can do without taking a lover. And anyway, if I did, you would be too much of a weakling for me." To this Reynard answered, "Milady, if I were favored, I would be more loving to you than a king who sought your love but tried to gain it in an unworthy manner."

At this point her husband, Isengrim, came back, and Reynard the courtier behaved as if they had not been speaking about anything much. Isengrim had returned empty-handed, and hunger had left him disconsolate. He told his wife how difficult it was to get hold of anything out in the fields. "I've never known it to be so bad," he said. "Every shepherd has a dog with him." [413–448]

CHAPTER 8

THE WOLF AND THE HAM

At this point Reynard spotted the farmer, and this promised to be a cause for rejoicing because he was carrying a large ham. Reynard laughed and said, "Listen to this, my Lord Isengrim!" "What's that, kinsman?" "Would you like to try some of that meat?" Isengrim and the family all declared that they would indeed.

Reynard got up and went over to a spot where he knew the farmer would have to pass, lifted up one foot, and began to limp heavily, and at the same time he bowed his back as if he had been beaten. The farmer yelled at him and dropped the ham onto the grass, because he was still after the white fur around Reynard's throat. He was carrying a fearsome-looking club. Reynard looked around, then lured him toward the forest. Isengrim jumped up, and before the farmer could do anything, he grabbed the ham and just as quickly started to gobble it up, forgetting entirely about Reynard. The farmer gave up the chase and wanted to retrieve his ham, but then he saw Isengrim, his nemesis, in the distance. He complained loud and long, but there was no sign of meat or bones, so he fell down on the grass and bewailed the loss of his ham.

Isengrim started to laugh. "Reynard's a good companion for me," he said. "We couldn't have gotten a better dinner, and it's all thanks to him." He had no idea, however, of where this would all lead in the end. Reynard came back with a smug look on his face and said, "Now where's my share?" Isengrim replied, "You'd better ask your kinswoman if she has saved any of hers."

"Sorry, Reynard," said the she-wolf, "I found it all far too tasty, but your reward will be in heaven! Don't be cross! It won't happen again." [449–498]

CHAPTER 9

THE WOLF AND THE WINE

"I'm really thirsty now," said Isengrim.

"How about some wine, my lord," said Reynard. "I can let you have a lot."

"If you can give me enough wine," said Isengrim, "I shall be your servant for life."

Reynard set off, with devious intentions, to a monastery that he knew about. Isengrim, the Lady Hirsent, and their sons went with him, and Reynard led them to a wine barrel, where Isengrim got drunk and began to sing in the manner of his forefathers, without thinking of any possible danger. The monks in charge of the wine said: "What's going on? I think we just heard a wolf." Right away six men came out, all armed with heavy batons, and Reynard quickly ran away. Hirsent and Isengrim now had to pay for the wine with a beating that was dealt out quite unmercifully. "If I get out of this," said Isengrim, "I swear I'll never touch a drop of wine again." They had really made a wrong call this time! The gate was barred, but they managed to jump over the fence and made their shameful escape. Isengrim complained bitterly about the shame and also the pain, since he was bruised all over. His wife had been thrashed, and his sons had had their share, too. They said, "Father, it has to be said that

that was an inappropriate song that you sang, and the whole affair was stupid."

Reynard came back and asked, "What is all this about?" Isengrim told him: "The four of us had to pay dearly for that wine, by God! On top of that my sons have cursed me, and that makes me very angry. I'm done with the pair of them!" Reynard smoothed things over. "Kinsman, calm down," he said. "I tell you, if one of my godsons has said something stupid, then it is not surprising, because he's still wet behind the ears." And then Reynard and Isengrim went their separate ways. [499–551]

CHAPTER 10

THE FOX AND THE ASS (INCOMPLETE)

Soon after this, Reynard came across Baldwin the ass, who was very heavily laden. His master had let him go on ahead. Reynard stopped him and said: "Baldwin, why do you put up with this? How can you live with such a heavy burden? If you come with me, I can rescue you from all this and can give you enough ..." [552–562 (There is a gap in the manuscripts here. The French texts do not have the incident, and it varies elsewhere, but in one known version, Baldwin is used in a complicated trick, which ends up, significantly, with Isengrim the wolf being castrated in a trap.)]

CHAPTER 11

KUNIN

Reynard left his kinsman. Isengrim, covered in blood, was on the point of death and said: "Alas for my life, and even more for my dear wife, who is noble and good and has always behaved decently and shunned any wickedness. Alas, too, for my sons, who will sadly now be fatherless, with only their mother left to bring them up. But I am comforted by the knowledge that my wife will not marry again."

The tree-goblin Kunin heard this complaint and asked, "What is the matter with you, Lord Isengrim?"

"I have been dreadfully wounded," he replied, "and I don't think I shall ever recover from this. And my dear wife will die of sorrow."

"No, she won't," said Kunin. "She hasn't been as chaste as you seem to be saying. I saw Reynard between her legs and at it, and this was not as much as a mealtime ago. Or isn't that sex? He was going in and out just like a shuttle."

Isengrim did not like what he was hearing and collapsed in sorrow, no longer knowing day from night. Kunin thought this was very funny. When Isengrim came to himself again, he said: "Goblin, I have a load of troubles, and now you are making it worse with your lying stories. If I were fool enough to believe them I would tear your eyes out. If you came down here, you wouldn't get up your tree ever again." But Kunin said, "You're a cuckold, you old fool!"

Isengrim howled. Suddenly Lady Hirsent appeared, and his sons with her. Isengrim was overjoyed to see them. With tears in his eyes, he said: "I have never been more pleased to see you, my sons, and my wife. I am done for, and that is the fault of Reynard—may he pay for it with his life! And on top of that, Kunin is driving me out of my mind by telling me wicked tales while I am sick—he said that Reynard had shared your bed. That story nearly killed me, although you should never believe what a liar tells you, and I did threaten to tear his eyes out."

"As God is my witness," said Lady Hirsent, "I haven't seen Reynard for three days. My lord Isengrim, I tell you, you must not say such foolish things." With that, Isengrim licked his wounds on both sides, and before long he was healed. [563–634]

CHAPTER 12

THE WOLF'S TONSURE

Reynard went back to his lair, afraid that he might get some unwelcome guests. He set up home in a cave in the forest and laid in a supply of food. One day, Isengrim came close to this lair in the forest. He was very unhappy and plagued by hunger, but another unpleasant adventure was in store for him.

Reynard was well provisioned and was in the process of cooking some eels, which Isengrim smelled. "Oho," he thought, "that must be a really good meal." The smell led him directly to his kinsman's door. Isengrim crouched down and hammered on it. Reynard, who could pull off amazing tricks, said: "Go away from my door! You must know that no one will come out and no one may come in at this time. What are you thinking of to behave like that! It is past the monastic hour of Nones, and we eremitical monks do not speak a word now, and would not do so even for all the gold of the Nibelungs."

"Kinsman," said Isengrim, "are you going to stay here as a monk until the end of your days?"

"Of course," replied Reynard. "I have no other choice, since through no fault of my own you have withdrawn your patronage and even wanted to take away my life."

"I will forgive you," said Isengrim, "for whatever harm you may have done to me, if you will just be my ally."

"You should indeed forgive me," said Reynard, "because my life would certainly be at stake if I ever tried tricking you. As a token of thanks, I can give you two pieces of cooked eel that I don't need today."

Isengrim was delighted by this and opened his mouth wide. Reynard threw in the pieces of eel, and Isengrim, fool that he was, said, "I would be more than happy if I could be the cook here."

"You could have plenty," said Reynard, "if you were to join our brotherhood. You could become the chief victualler."

This was not particularly good advice.

"I'll make the vows," said Isengrim. "So just put your head in here," said Reynard. Isengrim was happy to do so, but trouble was on the way. He put in his huge head, and Brother Reynard poured boiling water over it, burning off the hair and skin. Isengrim screamed.

"You surely didn't imagine that you could enter paradise in comfort? That would have betrayed great ignorance. You have to suffer the pain gladly, kinsman, and when you die, according to the rule of the order, a hundred thousand Masses will be said for you on one day. The Cistercians will then conduct you into heaven's glory, I am sure of it." [635–708]

CHAPTER 13

THE WOLF
GOES FISHING

Isengrim believed that this was true and did not worry too much about his hair and skin but said, "Kinsman, now that we are God's children, the eels must be communal property, so that anyone who denies me some would be in trouble with the Cistercians."

Reynard replied: "Of course. All that we have is available to you in fraternal love. We have, however, run out of fish. If you would care to come with me to where we have a fishpond, there are more fish there than can be counted. The brothers have stocked the pond."

"Let's go," said Isengrim.

They set off peaceably to the fishpond, which was frozen over. They had a look at the ice and discovered that a hole had been made in order to draw water. This would soon cause problems for Isengrim.

His supposed brother monk hated him with a passion, and Reynard was delighted to find a bucket that someone or other had left behind, and he tied it to Isengrim's tail.

"In nomine patris," said Isengrim, "what is that for?

"You have to lower the bucket into the hole, and I'll start the search. Just keep nice and still and we'll soon have loads of fish—I can see them through the ice."

Reynard was crafty, and Isengrim was not very bright. "Tell me, my brother in God's love, are there eels in there?"

"I've seen thousands of them!"

"Excellent. Let's catch them."

Isengrim was so dim-witted that he sat there, and his tail froze in. It was a cold and clear night, and his brother monk failed to warn him—Reynard didn't possess a scrap of loyalty—and so Isengrim's tail froze more and more securely in the ice.

"That bucket is getting heavy," said Isengrim.

"I've counted thirty eels in it already," replied Reynard. "This will be a profitable trip. If you just keep still, we can get a hundred of them."

Toward daybreak Reynard said: "I tell you, I'm afraid we shall have to abandon our greed for eels. I'm sorry to say that we have so many in the bucket that I can't catch any more. You will, sir, have trouble lifting it. See whether you can move it at all."

Isengrim started to pull, but his tail was held firmly in the ice, and he had to stay where he was.

"I'll go home and fetch our brother monks," said Reynard, "because we have had such good results."

By now it was full daylight, and Reynard made off. Isengrim the fisher, however, saw trouble coming. He spotted a mounted knight with his dogs, and they were on the trail of Isengrim, who began to regret his fishing expedition. The knight, who was out hunting, was called Sir Birtin, and this meant trouble for Lord Isengrim because the knight was now on his tracks. When Sir Birtin saw Isengrim, he shouted, "Go get him!" and urged the dogs on, and they began to tear at Isengrim.

Isengrim, who was now terrified, bit wildly. Sir Birtin caught up, drew his sword and quickly jumped down from his horse, then ran across the ice with his sword raised. The fisher-wolf was now less than happy that he had caught so much. But if you try to lift a load and can't carry it, then you will lose it all. And that is what happened to Isengrim.

Isengrim was surrounded. Sir Birtin had taken aim and was about to hack into the wolf's back and cut him in half when his feet skidded, and he fell. The slippery ice had made him unable to swing his sword. In spite of the fall, however, he did not give up, but came for Isengrim on his knees, but once again the ice did not allow him to swing his sword properly, and he only got Isengrim's tail, which he cut off completely.

This was bad for both of them. Sir Birtin bewailed the fact that he had missed his target, and Isengrim mourned the loss of his beloved tail, which was left behind as a hostage when he ran away. [709–822]

CHAPTER 14

THE FOX, THE WOLF, AND THE WELL

Reynard has told a great many lies, but today he is going to be tricked himself, although his innate cunning did get him out of a lot of trouble. He set off toward a monastery, where he knew they kept chickens, but things were, God knows, not as simple as all that for him, because the place had a very effective wall around it. Reynard had a look around and saw that by the gate was a large and deep well. He peered in, something he regretted later, because he saw his reflection in it, and now a very surprising thing happened. The creature whose cunning had worked wonders in the past now made a fool of himself. Reynard thought that what he was looking at was his wife, whom he loved more than life itself, even if he was unable to resist the urge to take a mistress (the pursuit of love is, after all, a delight for the soul, and this made her all the more desirable). Reynard smiled down, and the reflection moved. He was very thankful for this, and out of pure love he jumped into the well. He did this through the power of love, and for that he got wet to the ears.

He swam around in the well until he found a stone and rested his head on it. If you don't believe me, that's your problem!

God knows, Reynard thought that he had jumped to his death.

At this point, Lord Isengrim appeared (minus tail) out of the forest and headed for the monastery. He hadn't eaten, and I should say that he was keen to steal a sheep. By accident, then, he came by the well—something that would prove perilous for *him*!

Isengrim peered into the well, and I shall tell you what happened next. He saw his reflection in the water and he thought that his beloved wife, Hirsent, was down there. He pulled his head out and put it in again and the reflection on the water did the same, and this confused him completely. He began to complain to Lady Hirsent of all his pains and woes with loud howls, and as an answer his voice echoed in the hollow.

As soon became apparent, however, that well was actually full of trickery. "What's going on?" said Reynard.

Isengrim was going to be taken for a complete fool. "Is that you, brother Reynard?" he said. "I ask in all charity what you are doing there?"

"I am dead," came the reply, "but my soul is untroubled because you should know that I am in heaven. I am in charge of the heavenly school and am well suited to teaching children."

"Reynard, I am sorry to hear of your death."

"I am perfectly happy, though you still have to live with suffering every day down there in the world, while here in paradise I have more delights than anyone can imagine."

"My brother monk and kinsman," said Isengrim, "how is it that my lady Hirsent is there? I never went out on a raid without her taking part."

"She was redeemed," replied Reynard.

"So tell me, my dear kinsman, how she comes to be so burned around the head."

"I shall tell you, my dear fellow. She had a taste of hell—you will often have heard that no one can enter paradise without having seen hell, and that is where she lost the hair on her head."

Reynard was keen to get out of the well, and at this point Isengrim saw his eyes. "Tell me, my brother monk," he said, "what are those shining lights?" "Those are precious jewels," replied Reynard, "pure red gemstones that shine with a light that you don't see outside. There are cows and pigs here, too, and the fattest sheep, all wandering around without a shepherd—everything that could be desired."

"If only I could get there, too," said Isengrim foolishly.

"Just follow my instruction—I shall show you, on my honor, so just listen carefully. You will need to sit in the bucket."

The arrangement at the well was that when one bucket was lowered, the other one came up. Without hesitation, Isengrim did as his kinsman asked; he stretched, fool that he was, and stepped into the bucket. Reynard, concerned with himself, got into the lower bucket.

To his misfortune, Isengrim met his kinsmen right at the midpoint. "Brother Reynard," said Isengrim, "what did your words mean?"

"I shall tell you the truth. You will be taking over my place here in heaven, which I give you gladly. I want to go back to the earth, and you are going directly into the devil's hands." Isengrim sank to the bottom, and Reynard escaped unscathed to the forest.

The well was almost completely drained. Had this not been the case it would have been the end of Isengrim, who didn't think much of paradise and would gladly have been out of there.

The monks needed to draw some water, and one of the brothers now came along. He tugged on the rope, but the bucket seemed to be much heavier than it had ever been. He leaned over the well to try and see what the problem was, and there he saw Isengrim sitting at the bottom of the well in a bucket. Without a moment's delay he ran back to the monastery as fast as he possibly could and told them the amazing story of what was in the well. "I saw Isengrim!" "It's the judgment of God upon him," shouted the monks, and off they all ran, which put Isengrim in a lot of danger.

The prior took a long and heavy club, and one of the others took a candlestick, and there was a lot of noise. "Mind he doesn't get out," they all cried. They turned the wheel that pulled up the rope, and the foolish Isengrim was quickly brought to the top. Reynard had really deceived him! The prior came close to killing Isengrim, who had to suffer the beating.

Reynard had played a good number of tricks on Isengrim, to be sure, and one wonders what the wolf could have been thinking to let himself be deceived so often. The world is always the same, however—someone who lies and cheats gets on better than someone who keeps his word, and it will stay like that for many a long day. Plenty of people think that cheating is the thing to do nowadays. God knows, there are some people, both young and old, who think that no one has ever been tricked as wickedly as they. But none of us has ever been so badly treated that they don't find out that the same thing has happened to someone else as well.

Isengrim was now in a terrible position, and they were going to finish him off. Then the prior noticed his tonsure and said to the monks: "We've done a very wicked deed! I've just spotted that he has a tonsure, and I'll tell you something else—this wolf Isengrim has been circumcised according to Old Testament law. Oh Lord, we should not have delivered all those blows, because he is obviously a penitent."

The monks said: "Well, it's done now. It's just a pity we didn't notice that before." And with that, they left.

If Isengrim had not lost his tail and been given a tonsure, those men of God would have strung him up.

The nobleman Walther von Horburg always used to say whenever something bad happened to him, "Even if I have to suffer, I'll get some good out of it in the end." And that was the case with Isengrim. [823–1030]

CHAPTER 15

A DAY IN COURT

When the monks had gone, Isengrim crept back into the forest and began to howl. When Lady Hirsent heard this, she hurried to him with his two sons, and Isengrim complained bitterly: "My dear sons, my dear wife," he said, "because of Reynard my life is worthless. In God's name let it be a cause of anger to you. It is Reynard's fault that I am lacking a tail, and without any provocation from me his trickery led me toward my death, and I have been beaten and battered because of his extreme disloyalty."

The companionship with him was at an end, and now Reynard's former patron was an enemy. The wolves all wept bitterly, and Isengrim was distressed by this. "Lady Hirsent," he said, "my dear wife, this mars your great beauty. Your tears cause me pain, so for God's sake, desist!"

"Alas, I cannot go on. It is great sorrow to me that my husband no longer has a tail! How can I survive, poor creature that I am!"

And so the great feud began. Isengrim trotted off to look for Reynard. He took up a position where he could lie in wait, because anyone who starts an open feud without preparation will need a lot of cunning to save himself.

This is how the feud got under way. A lynx soon heard about it, and he was affected by this quarrel, because he had strong ties to both sides, to the wolves and to the fox. The lynx, therefore, was worried and said to Isengrim: "My kinsman, Lord Isengrim, of what are you accusing my cousin? You are both related to me, and I could act as an arbitrator if you will explain your complaint about what Reynard has done. Then we can set a trial date, and he can answer for it in court."

"Listen, my dear kinsman," said Isengrim, "it is a long story, because I have a lot to complain about with all the things Reynard has done to me. It is down to him that I am deprived of a tail, and he has been trying it on with my wife. If he were at least innocent of that, I would let him off for the other matters. But I agree with you—I want a day in court."

A day was settled upon, three weeks from then. Isengrim appeared and brought with him many of his kinsmen and friends. I'll tell you about some of them, and you will certainly know them. The elephant was there, and the bison, both seeming like giants to Reynard, then the stag Randolt and the hind, both friends of Isengrim. Bruin the bear and also the boar—they both wanted to support Isengrim. It is not appropriate for me to name all of them, but every one of the large beasts was with Isengrim, though they might have been better off elsewhere.

Reynard had Grimbard the badger on his side, and he was useful—he had never left Reynard in the lurch, nor did he ever do so until the day they both died. The hare, the rabbit, and other little animals—which I shall not enumerate—came along in large numbers.

Isengrim had given thought to the matter and brought with him Lord Reize, who was a ferocious hound, on whose teeth—this was Bruin's suggestion—Reynard's innocence should be tested. Reize was made to lie still as if dead, something that very nearly outwitted the ever-cunning Reynard. Grimbard, however, noticed Reize lying there and said: "Reynard, don't ignore me but listen, because it's true—Reize will bite you to death. If you step too close to his mouth that will be the end of you."

The lynx, who had brought them all together, said to Reynard, "Take note that you must in our presence give Isengrim formal assurance that you have not made advances upon his wife."

"I shall do so," he replied, "on my life, and in such a way as he will himself acknowledge it. If only," he went on, "the whole world were as free of lies and falsehood as I have always been!"

With that, Reynard went to consult his supporters, and he sent them away. "Do you know what I noticed?" he asked. "Reize the hound is alive, and so I am getting out of here—may God preserve all of you!"

Reynard leaped into the open field, and many of the wild beasts shouted: "Look out! Reynard is on the run!" Isengrim was furious and chased off after him, though the Lady Hersint was way ahead of him, which was not, in the event, a good move. She wanted to bite her suitor to death to prove her own innocence and for the sake of Isengrim. Reynard, however, was good at false trails and craftily waved his tail just in front of her mouth, then ran to his fortress, which was a nicely hollowed badgers' sett, of the sort that foxes often run off to, even now. This saved him. [1031–1167]

CHAPTER 16

THE RAPE OF THE SHE-WOLF

Lady Hersint chased him into the burrow, but only her front part went in, and this would be a great cause of shame for her. She could neither move forward nor go back, and Reynard took full advantage of this situation. He rushed out of another hole in the burrow, jumped up onto his kinswoman and coupled with her. Isengrim saw this happening before his eyes, and it broke his heart.

"Dearest," said Reynard, "from now on, you should stay with me. In God's name no one knows about it, and for the sake of your reputation I shall keep quiet about it."

The shame felt by Lady Hersint was enormous. In her fury she bit on stones, but her great strength could not help her. At this point Reynard saw Isengrim coming, wild with anger. "I think I had better get away," said Reynard, and went back into the burrow.

Isengrim had his sons with him, and a lot of fearsome animals came, too, and Isengrim was able to testify to them that his beloved wife had been raped. Isengrim wept, and Hersint was pulled free by her back legs. "Reynard had tricked me countless times," declared Isengrim, "but I could let them all pass except for this shame, which I was forced to see. That is just too much."

Reynard came to the door of the lair and said: "I have done you no harm. My kinswoman wanted to come in and I welcomed her. My patron can testify that I did nothing to him."

"In all truth," replied his relative and patron, "I can no longer be your sponsor. I have no choice but to be your enemy, and your death shall be by my hand."

"No, no, my patron," said Reynard, "that would not be a sensible move. You would not get away with it, and you would spend all your time in chains."

"My lady Hersint," said Isengrim, "in truth it has been seven years since I first took you as my wife. Many fine beasts from both of our families were present, and since then we have been completely happy together. But now Reynard has brought shame upon us—alas that we ever accepted him as a family member. I shall regret that forever."

Lady Hersint wept, and Isengrim howled, and his sons with him. Burdened with shame they trotted away, filled with anger.

"Most noble kinsman," said Reynard, "my dear Lord Isengrim, you ought to stay here. But if, my lord, you really want to go, then leave my kinswoman here. She is the real mistress of this house!"

Isengrim made no reply. [1168–1238]

CHAPTER 17

THE ANTS AND THE LION

All these events took place during an established time of peace and the rule of law, imposed, on pain of death by hanging, by a lion named Noble, who held sway over the whole land. No other beast could resort to any kind of violence without being brought to trial before him. Everyone obeyed him, and he was their ruler under God. He was, however, forced to impose the rule of law, because he thought that he was with some certainty facing a grim death. I shall now tell you why.

Noble went to an anthill and told the ants to stand still, and then he informed them, to their surprise, that he was their overlord. They had no intention of becoming his subjects, and this made him very angry. In a rage he leaped onto their fortress and battled with the little animals, because he thought that was the thing to do. More than a thousand of them lay dead, and many more were seriously wounded, but a good number of them survived. Noble took out his fury on them and brought down their fortress to its foundations. He had done them an immeasurable amount of damage, and then he went on his way. The ants bewailed their situation and told of the great suffering inflicted on their people. Their happiness had been destroyed on this most sorrowful of days.

The ruler of that fortress, however, was a fierce and wild ant. When he returned from a trip into the forest he learned with horror of the great pains suffered by his people. "Who did this to you?" he asked. Those who had survived complained bitterly about their distress. "Our loyalty brought this upon us, Noble told us that we were to be subject to him, but we wanted no other ruler than you, and for that we had to suffer. He killed vast numbers of our people, and he destroyed this fortress. If this deed goes unavenged, then we shall be forever dishonored."

"I would sooner die," replied their leader, and at once set off in search of the lion, whom he found asleep under a linden tree. The ruler of the ants went grimly up to him. "God in heaven," he thought, "how can I get revenge for my people? Even if I bite him to death I shan't be able to drag him away." He thought and thought, and then gathered up his strength and jumped into Noble's ear, which would cause problems for the lion.

Reynard—who was hidden nearby—saw all this.

People say that is it unwise to underestimate your enemies, and the lion was made to suffer for doing so. The ant made straight for his brain. The king recoiled in shock and said: "Merciful God, what is this horrible feeling? Alas, I wish I had refrained from that kind of action because now I am in misery! I shall not do it again." The lion screamed loudly, and many of the beasts heard him and came running. "What has happened?" they asked. "I'm in pain," he replied, "I can tell you that much—it must be a punishment from God on me for not holding a formal trial." [1239–1320]

CHAPTER 18

THE GREAT ASSEMBLY AND THE SAINTLY CHICKEN

Straightaway the lion gave orders for a formal assembly, and envoys were sent to the farthest parts of the empire. It was fixed to take place in a certain meadow, six weeks from then. There could be no refusal. Seating for the participants was duly erected, at a cost of more than a thousand silver pieces.

Let me tell you who attended the court. From what I heard, the first to come were the panther and the elephant, the ostrich and the famous bison. The assembly was a very large one. There was the sable and the pine marten, the swift leopard in his headdress, the stag and the bear, the mouse and the mole, the rabbit and the stoat, the lynx and the deer, the billy goat and the ram. The ibex hurried down from the mountains, and the hare and the boar came from the forest with the otter and the marmot. The camel came, too, and a crowd of beavers and hedgehogs, the stoat and the squirrel—none of these wanted to miss the assembly. The aurochs came, as well as Kunin the goblin, the stallion, Baldwin the ass, the hound Reize, and the bull seal from the sea, Grimbard the badger, and a great many more animals that I cannot list because I never heard all the details of them. Isengrim, Lady Hersint, and their sons were there as well. The king took his place at the throne of judgment. Reynard was not at court, but he still managed to cause harm to some of his enemies.

The king gave orders that they should all quiet down. Isengrim then demanded justice for himself. He asked for an advocate, to which the king agreed, and it was to be Bruin the bear. Bruin said, "My lord, Isengrim requests by rights of law and by your grace that if I defend him badly, I may be relieved and replaced." "Granted," replied the king.

"Most mighty and magnificent king, the lord Isengrim wishes to make before you a complaint regarding his shame and harm. That he stands before you today without a tail is because of Reynard. This shames Isengrim terribly. Reynard also violated his noble wife, the Lady Hersint, and did so during the time of peace and the rule of law that you imposed on pain of death by hanging. This was a crime against you."

Grimbard now stepped forward and said: "Your Majesty, hear my words, too. This statement is unreliable and may well be a lie. How could my client have violated her? The Lady Hersint is bigger than he is. If, however, he did lie with her and make love to her, this is not a great surprise—such things happen all the time. No one around here knew about it. Lady Hersint, perhaps *you* could tell us why your husband is telling this tale about you. Surely this is hard on you, and very difficult for your sons, who are fine young lads. I find the complaint, in all honesty, vexatious. Your majesty, examine closely just what damage he has sustained. If Lord Isengrim's wife has really been besmirched by Reynard, even in the tiniest respect, I shall still support my kinsman."

Isengrim raised his complaint once more and said, "My lords, I declare before you all that the actual harm done to me bothers me only half as much as the shame."

The king called upon the stag for a decision under oath about which side was in the right.

THE GREAT ASSEMBLY AND THE SAINTLY CHICKEN

Randolt spoke. "The lord Isengrim has suffered much shame—this cannot be denied—indeed, an excess of it. He should have been spared Reynard's trickery. This reflects badly upon your majesty. And if he violates noble ladies, well then, how can he be allowed to live? On my oath I condemn him on my understanding alone and without any personal involvement in the matter. You should arrest him, and if you can take him, you should give orders that he be hanged as swiftly as possible. That way your own honor will be preserved."

The king was just as angry. "My lords," he asked, "are you in agreement?" They all said "yes," since they were very keen on seeing Reynard suffer.

No one raised an objection apart from a camel from Tusculum, who was both pious and wise, and gray with age. She placed her feet together in front of her and said: "Your majesty, hear me, too. I hear many worthy souls making a judgment that seems to me to be unjust. Perhaps they are not understanding the matter correctly. On my oath, sir, I shall attempt to put you right. If a complaint is made against someone in this assembly, and he is not present, he must be informed, and should be summoned formally three times. If he fails to appear, this is to be counted against him, and his life is forfeit. That is my judgment under oath." Isengrim was unhappy about this, but all the animals, large and small, agreed with the camel, and that was how the debate ended.

Now Chantecler appeared, with his wife, Pinte, and on a bier they carried their dead daughter. This was their complaint: that on that very day she had been killed by Reynard the red fox. The bier was set down before the king, who felt great shame, but Isengrim was pleased by this.

Chantecler began his speech of complaint. "Your majesty," he said, "hear what I have to say. You must surely now realize that Reynard is mocking your entire kingdom, and he has continued to do so. Alas, he has bitten to death my most precious daughter!"

The king become very angry indeed, much distressed by this complaint. "By my beard," he declared, "Reynard the Fox must certainly leave this land, or his life will be forfeit."

The hare saw how angry the king was and was afraid (cowardly as all hares are) for his own life. He trembled and shook with anxiety.

The king ordered that a Mass be sung by his chaplain, Bruin the bear, and his scholar-choristers. The dead chicken was soon laid to rest. The hare, however, lay down on her grave and went to sleep. This proved lucky for him, and I shall tell you why: it cured him of his trembling and shaking. When he awoke he went to the king and told him that this was a great miracle, and that the chicken was sanctified in the sight of God. This story spread, and all agreed that it was indeed a sign, and they all sang a great hymn of praise.

Reynard was given no credit for his part—in fact, everyone demanded that the mighty king should make a firm judgment regarding this evil deed. "Before our very eyes," they said, "God has given us a sign. Reynard should never have martyred this blameless saint." [1321–1510]

CHAPTER 19

THE BEAR AND THE HONEY

The king gave orders to his chaplain, Sir Bruin, to go and find Reynard. He was inclined to refuse for fear of danger, but did what the king had commanded, and went looking for him in the forest. Reynard's cunning, however, was boundless, and the whole of the land suffered for it. Bruin found Reynard by his lair, a cave in a stony cliff, where he was safe from his enemies. The cave is still to this day called "The Hell-Hole."

Reynard knew how he should receive the great king's chaplain. "Welcome, most noble cleric," he said. "Come, tell me how things are at court. I know that you are one of the king's counselors."

"Heavy charges have been laid against you. If your honor means anything to you, then come to the court and answer to them. This is what the great king has ordered."

"Sir Chaplain," replied Reynard, "let us have something to eat, and then we shall be better prepared to go to the court." Reynard's honesty here was somewhat questionable. "I know a tree full of the best honey."

"Right, let's go! That's always my favorite."

Sir Bruin went off with Reynard, who took him to a place where a farmer had hammered a wedge into a split tree trunk. It was devilish to take Bruin there. "Sir Chaplain, my dear friend, you may help yourself, but be careful—there are lots of bees."

Unconcerned about the bees, the bear just stuck his head into the split trunk. Reynard pulled out the wedge, and the sides snapped together and trapped the chaplain. This was going to be a long meal!

"Ow!" shouted Sir Bruin. "What's the matter?" asked Reynard. "I did warn you, and now the bees are going to get you. Enjoy your dinner! The king is so powerful that he'll probably be able to get back at me." And off he went.

The court chaplain bewailed his situation, but then he heard the sound of a wagon coming, which frightened him, and he pulled backward hard to try to escape. When the wagoner spotted him, he kept very quiet until he was back in the village. Then he ran to the church, took hold of the bell rope, and the noise was heard all over, so that everyone who heard it came rushing into the village. The farmer told them the story, that there was a bear trapped in his split tree trunk. "God has helped us! I can show you where it is."

They all, men and women alike, set out, and dreadful things happened. One bold young coxcomb was the first to get to Bruin. He was holding a club. The lion's chaplain heard the hullabaloo and was very frightened indeed. He set his feet against the tree trunk and pulled free, but he left behind both ears and the skin of his head. The honey did not seem quite so desirable now.

The royal envoy made his escape, but there was insult upon injury. Reynard, never one to avoid malice, was sitting by his lair, and when he saw Sir Bruin in his hairless state, he called out to him. What he said was: "My good Sir Chaplain, what happened to your skullcap? Did you pawn it to buy wine? Oh dear, I shall be most ashamed if they say at court that I have been an ungenerous host."

Sir Bruin returned in his shorn state to the court and complained bitterly. The other animals, old and young, came along and saw his large bald patch. As court chaplain he poured out his bitter sorrow to the king himself. "Reynard did this," he said. "My lord, I ordered him to appear before your majesty, but look how he treated me! I would rather be dead!"

The king was furious at what had happened to his beloved chaplain and became very depressed. Straightaway he asked the beaver what the right thing was to do. "My lord," he replied, "there is no alternative. He must be condemned, and his life and property must be forfeit, and if anyone aids or abets him, they should be outlawed. That is my judgment on oath." Randolt the stag said, "That is just," and many other loyal followers agreed.

The elephant, however, was angry and said: "I cannot agree to that. A judgment has already been made—you all heard it—and that cannot be changed. An envoy must be sent to summon him up to three times. The devil take anyone who causes harm by betraying what has been sworn." This was accepted, and Tibert the cat would suffer in consequence. [1511–1646]

CHAPTER 20

THE TOMCAT AND THE MICE

The king summoned Tibert and told him to go and find Reynard. "My lord," he said, "I can legitimately refuse to do so, because he is a cherished kinsman." "You cannot refuse this commission on any grounds," declared Randolt. "After all, you are not all that fond of him." The king ordered him to do it on his life, and Tibert said, "Well, it's time to go," and he set off hurriedly.

In the forest he met his kinsman Reynard, that master of all kinds of wickedness, and I'll tell you what Reynard said when he saw Tibert. "Welcome, my blood brother and relative! It pains me to the heart that you have been avoiding me. Never have I had a more welcome guest."

"Thank you," replied Tibert. "I thought, too, that it had been a long time. The king sent me to you, and he swore a solemn oath that you will have to leave the country if you do not present yourself before him. Everyone is making complaints about you, and you did indeed do very wrong when you sent the court chaplain back after he had been scalped."

"My friend," replied Reynard, "in all truth I have not laid eyes on Sir Bruin at all this year except once, when Isengrim was on my heels. But what do you say to this, friend and kinsman—come with me and I will share with you all that I possess. I have a house here in the neighborhood that is empty, and in which I keep a supply of mice for my guests, so please help yourself to the best of them!"

It was a bright and clear night, and Reynard was about to trick the tomcat. He led him to that house, and Tibert was most eager to eat. In the house there lived a priest, on whom Reynard had played many of his tricks, and now Tibert would be paying for them.

The priest had put a noose of cord as a trap around an entry-hole—people still do that quite often—and it was intended for Reynard, although it would put his friend in peril. Tibert was eager to get in and fell straight into the trap. The priest's housekeeper heard this and shouted: "Up! Up, upon my soul!" The startled priest sat up, took a knife and got up and went toward Tibert, though he thought it was Reynard. Tibert was not happy about the situation and screamed as loudly as he could. Because it was dark, the priest only cut the noose away. Tibert was keen to escape, which he very quickly managed—he got out and ran for it.

The priest's housekeeper, who had stayed inside, now caused mayhem. She smacked the priest's head with her open hand, then grabbed a piece of wood and beat him black and blue with it. Had it not been for the intervention of Werburga, the maid, it would have been the end of him. "God delivered Reynard up," said the housekeeper, "and you took him from me!" "My dear lady, I was unlucky," said the bruised priest, "but do please forgive me!"

Tibert abandoned the mice and was eager to get away. All through that night he ran with all his strength to get back to the court. Early next morning he reached the king and appeared before him with the noose still around his neck. Tibert complained bitterly about Reynard: "Your majesty, I was in great peril. Because of your summons, Reynard wanted to kill me. I survived only by the grace of God. My lord, neither your chaplain nor I will go and summon him again." [1647–1742]

CHAPTER 21

THE BADGER, THE FOX, AND THE SICK LION

The king was saddened by their complaints, and at the same time he was feeling ill, but mostly he was very angry. He asked the boar for his opinion on the right way to proceed, now that the envoys Bruin and Tibert had been so unjustly mistreated. The boar was equally incensed. "He should be stripped of his honor and property, and he should be banished, his wife declared a widow and his children orphans." "I agree!" said Isengrim. The king then asked everyone—wise or unwise—if they were in agreement.

Grimbard the badger did not hide his thoughts. "Most noble Majesty," he said, "if Sir Bruin lost his scalp without it being the fault of my relative, then your anger is misplaced. Tibert, too, may also be in the wrong, because he hates Reynard. Therefore, it is clear that no one should make such a judgment, because it might damage your own esteem or weaken the power of the court by making it a laughingstock. There must be no corruption. My kinsman must be summoned one more time." "You must go yourself," said the king. "I give you this commission on your life. If God will, then your kinsman may accept you as an envoy."

Everyone laughed, but Grimbard was not particularly worried, and went quickly off to the forest in search of his kinsman.

* * *

The story gets really strange and interesting here, and it is being told to you in all truth by a storyteller named Heinrich, who put together the book of Isengrim's struggles. If you don't believe all this, then you can keep your money. But now let's go back to where we left off.

* * *

Grimbard made his way to Reynard's fortress, and the fox was very pleased to see him. He said, with a laugh, "Welcome, my kinsman! Come and tell me what I am being accused of at court."

"The mighty king is threatening with dreadful penalties," replied Grimbard. "He has heard a lot of complaints against you, and if you don't appear before him this very day, you will have to flee the country, or you'll die. But if you do turn up in court, and Isengrim sees you, you will be condemned by everyone."

"I'm not going to let that put me off," said Reynard. "I shan't be blamed for anything else." Then they sat down and had a meal.

Once the table had been cleared, Reynard got up and swiftly disappeared into his room and fetched what he would wear to court, the best clothing that he had; namely, a linen pilgrim's robe. He put it on and took up a physician's bag—no one could ever estimate the extent of Reynard's cunning—and off he went. He was carrying packets of cloves and cinnamon as if he were a doctor, and he also had a number of unknown roots and herbs. He took up a staff, and he and his kinsmen went quickly from the forest to the court. He crossed himself and said, "May God preserve me from wicked calumny, that those who lie may not hurt me."

When Reynard arrived at court, many of the wild animals said to themselves: "Now we shall see something interesting, how Reynard gets on—he has made a mockery of so many animals. He is Lady Hersint's lover, and if they were both to be hanged from the same branch, no one should complain. Why did the villain pick her?"

The angry masses rightly clamored against him. Isengrim complained strongly that his wife had been dishonored. Then the chaplain said, "He did me a lot of harm as well." "Your Majesty," said Tibert, "just look at him standing there, when he has brought so much shame upon you. Don't let him get away. You should have him hanged, because without any doubt he is a traitor." Chantecler complained about the loss of his daughter: "My lord king, we all know that you are a just judge over us, and therefore it would be very bad indeed if you allow this murderer to live. He should be hanged at once." Dizelin the crow said, "My lord, hang my so-called friend."

Reynard's cunning was limitless. "O King," he said, "what is all this noise about? I've visited lots of courts but I've never encountered such unruly behavior. Really, I am sorry for you."

"Right," said the king, and the shouting was stopped.

"Your Majesty," said Reynard, "Doctor Pendin, a surgeon from Salerno, offers you his service, since he is concerned—as are all of them there, old or young—about your esteem and standing. If anything should happen to you, they would not be able to cope. My lord, I was in Salerno because I greatly desire to help you to recover from your illness. I am well aware that all your problems, whatever they may be, have to do with your head. Doctor Pendin instructs me to tell you to take every day these medicaments that he has sent you."

"I shall do so," said the king, whose anger had evaporated.

"In the past seven weeks," said Reynard, "I have had many a thorn in my feet, and it has been a painful time. The surgeon also recommends that if you can find an old wolf, you should skin it. Furthermore, you need the skin of a bear." "That will have to be the chaplain," said the king.

"Those things will cure you, my dear lord. And in addition, you absolutely have to have a cap made of catskin, because without that, as God's my witness, you will die."

Hearing this, the king summoned Isengrim and his chaplain. "He will have to give me your skins," he said, "and I shall be indebted to you, and your families, forever. Master Reynard has explained all about the illness that is raging so painfully in my head."

"Have mercy, my lord," said Bruin the chaplain. "What on earth is going on? That fellow you take to be a doctor has caused plenty more deaths, God knows, than he has ever healed. Besides, you have already condemned him." Lord Isengrim then said to him, "If this is the way you pass judgment regarding my wife, then things are bad." He showed the stump of his tail and continued: "Look what damage your doctor caused to my rear end. The same thing might happen to you."

Sir Bruin and Isengrim wished themselves far away from there, but that was impossible—they were unable to escape. The king had them seized by a number of strong guards, and they were skinned, as was Tibert, too.

That was all Reynard's doing, and he said: "Well done. What we need now is a chicken, cooked with boar fat." "That will have to be Lady Pinte," said the king, and summoned Chantecler. "I need your wife as medication."

"No, no, my lord! She is dearer to me than life itself. Eat me and let her live."

"That would not work," said Reynard.

The king had Pinte caught, and Chantecler ran off. According to what had been decreed, they now took an extremely large slice of fat from the boar, who was very unhappy with this medical procedure.

"And we also need a strip of deer hide."

The king summoned the stag and said, "Randolt, you are to provide me with a belt, and I shall be forever grateful."

"Lord, in God's name spare me," said the stag. "It's a complete mockery that you are listening to someone who could never be trusted. If he is supposed to be a doctor, then it was the devil who taught him medicine."

"Randolt," said the king, "You have always held me dear, and if I die and it is your fault, you would regret it forever." The stag did not dare refuse the king, and provided a belt cut from his hide, from nose to tail.

Reynard had stormed his way over them all, and the wonderworking fox now said: "My king, if you were a poor man I should not be able to help you. But by the grace of God we have the means to cure you, as long as you follow my instructions." "Of course," replied the king. "I shall do whatever you tell me, doctor."

Reynard was extremely crafty. "My master, Pendin, asks for no payment other than a beaver pelt." "And he shall have it," said the mighty king. "I shall send him one." He summoned the beaver and demanded his skin. A lot of the animals watched this and said to each other: "What might happen to us? We had better get out of here before we all lose our skins." Many bold beasts left, and the court was emptied.

Grimbard was still there, however, and the camel from Tusculum. The doctor let them stay, and also the elephant, who had judged in his favor. The great king was left alone with only his immediate circle when almost all the others fled.

Reynard told the king to have a bath prepared, and he gave orders for this at once. The leopard hurried to the task—I am telling you the honest truth—and the nice warm bath was quickly brought in by faithful servants, all as Doctor Reynard had prescribed. They were all worried that their lord might die. Reynard put plenty of herbs into the bath, then carefully put the catskin cap on the king's head and made him step into the bath. Master Reynard the doctor touched a vein that led to the

THE BADGER, THE FOX, AND THE SICK LION

king's heart and said: "My king, you are cured. You have good cause to rejoice, because you were very near to death, but my skill has saved you from great peril. Get out of the bath," went on the doctor, "you have bathed long enough. Too long a bath can weaken a sick person, and you are looking a little pale."

The king, like a sick man eager to be cured, said, "I shall do whatever you say." He was then bedded down comfortably on the bearskin taken from his formerly much-loved chaplain, and Reynard covered him up warmly with—God help us!—the skin that had belonged to Isengrim, and that he had lost through no fault of his own.

Reynard really was very cunning. He now put hot poultices on the king's head. The ant felt this, left the king's brain, and crawled into the fur of the catskin cap. The doctor took the skin outside and let the sun shine on it, which had a great effect. He now saw the ant and said to him angrily: "Ant, you shall die! You have caused great sorrow to my lord, and that will cost you your life."

The ant replied: "I had to do it—this mighty king wrecked my fine castle. This was a great hardship, about which I can never complain enough. Many of my kinsmen were slain, and that is why I did this. If you let me live, I shall give you the power to rule over a thousand fortresses in my forest."

Reynard thought this was a good resolution and at once released the captive ant. The ant was very pleased and went off back into the forest. Had he not agreed to the deal, he would have been killed. This sort of thing happens all the time. If someone can pay up, he will do much better than if he tries to act according to the word of the Lord—God help us!

Reynard went back to where he had left his patient. He felt the king's brow and said, "How does your head feel, my lord?"

"Very well, master, and may God reward you for it—you have certainly cured me!" "There are still some things to do," said Reynard. "Does anyone know whether the chicken was cooked with parsley?" A chamberlain was standing by, and he replied, "Yes, certainly." "Then have it brought in." This was soon done, and Reynard invited his lord to eat, and let him spoon up the broth. His doctor did not delay in eating up Lady Pinte himself. Reynard, faithless wretch that he was, gave Grimbard the boar fat. Then he permitted the king to get up and walk about a little. [1743–2096]

CHAPTER 22

THE ELEPHANT AND THE CAMEL

Reynard, who rarely showed any loyalty to anyone, pressed the king to confer upon his friend, the elephant, lordship over a country. "Granted," said the king. "Let him rule Bohemia." This pleased the elephant very much, and the king gave it to him to hold in fief in accordance with the law. The good servant of the king set off at once. He had come poor to the court and was now a prince. The elephant traveled to the land where the king had sent him and announced to the people the surprising news that he was now their overlord. For this he was severely beaten and had to go back in sorrow to where he came from. They might easily have wounded him so severely that he would not have survived.

Having had the elephant made ruler of a country, Reynard thought that he still hadn't exercised enough malice. Again he made an urgent request to the king about the camel, who had been one of those judging him. "She should also play a useful role," he said. "Make her the abbess at Erstein in Alsace, and this will save your soul, because they send up a lot of prayers." The king acceded gladly to the request and granted her with his right hand a role that would be financially very beneficial to her. Certainly she saw herself as a wealthy and powerful abbess, so she took her leave and hurried to take up the post.

She skipped gaily across the courtyard and was very grateful to Reynard for the gift of this important position. It would, however, lead to trouble for her. When she reached the convent, all those who had heard the news hurried along. They looked at her and immediately wanted to know who she was. "I shall give you an honest answer," she said. "The mighty king has granted me authority over this place. I shall be the abbess." The nuns were so angry about this that the camel was nearly killed. The nuns closed in on her, and the abbess was beaten to within an inch of her life. They used their sharp writing implements to make wounds on her body, and it put her in a great deal of danger. The nuns chased her into the Rhine, and that was the reward she got for speaking in Reynard's favor. This, too, happens all the time. If you try and help a scoundrel out of his difficulties, all you will get out of it is wickedness. We have seen it often enough, and we shall see it happening again and again.

That, then, was how Reynard treated all those who had been involved in judging him. [2097–2156]

CHAPTER 23

THE MURDER OF THE KING

Reynard the doctor was so wicked that he very soon betrayed the king. He had a great many malicious tricks up his sleeve. "My lord," he said, "I shall give you a drink that will restore you completely." "Do so," replied the king. But what he brewed was death to the king. Reynard the red fox was evil, and he now made it very clear indeed: he poisoned his lord.

No one should protest about this too much. What, after all, did anyone expect of Reynard? God knows, it is disgraceful that at court there are plenty of scoundrels who are held in greater esteem than those who have never acted dishonorably. If a ruler dies because of needlessly following someone like that, then that is all to the good. Unfortunately, wicked deceivers seem to come to the fore every time, and the honest ones are left outside.

When the king had taken the drink, Reynard left, saying he had to go and search for herbs and roots. He had simply done as he always did. He took the hand of his dear kinsman Grimbard and said: "I want to tell you something. The king cannot be cured, and we should not stay here any longer." Together they hurried off into the forest, where Reynard saw Sir Bruin the chaplain wandering around without his bearskin. I'll tell you what the fox said when he saw him. "Most noble cleric, was your fur so heavy that I must see you skinless? Quite honestly, I should think that if, come winter, you have to represent anyone in court, you'll have to borrow a fur coat. No one can deny that you certainly need one. Oh dear, who took your skin away?"

Sir Bruin was so angry that he could not say a word. He was less than happy to see Reynard, and his fury was palpable. He growled and bared his teeth, and Reynard left Sir Bruin there and went back to his lair.

The king was in a great deal of pain. "Where is Doctor Reynard?" he said. "Send for him to come quickly. Something horrible is happening to me—I have no idea what—but it is piercing me to the heart. He will be able to sort it out, with his wonderful herbs. He is a most excellent physician."

They looked for the doctor, but the king was very distressed when they told him that he had unfortunately gone away. Weeping, the king said: "The fact that I ever met Reynard has cost me my life. Alack and alas, he has poisoned me, without any fault on my side. I have never done him any harm. At his behest I had my noble chaplain skinned. If you rely on someone who is untrustworthy, I can only say that it will end in sorrow. That is what happened to me." The king turned his face to the wall, and then he died. His head split into three parts and his tongue into nine. Everyone had to weep for the death of the noble king.

And they all vigorously cursed Reynard the Fox.

* * *

Whether all this is true or not, let us hope that God will give us a good year! This is the end of the tale, which was composed by Heinrich the Storyteller, although his rhymes were sometimes uneven, so that someone else—someone equally good with narrative—tidied it up. In doing so, he left the actual story as it was, although in some lines he put in material that was not there before, and he left out other parts that seemed to be too wordy. If you want to reward him, pray that God should grant him a happy life and afterward receive his soul in that place where joys are never-ending. Amen. [2157–2266]

Printed in the United States
by Baker & Taylor Publisher Services